I0558892

BLUE KINGDOMS

Zombies, Werewolves, & Unicorns

~ TWO PULSE-POUNDING NOVELLAS ~

Stephen D. Sullivan

Walkabout Publishing • 2011

This book is a work of fiction. Any references to historical events, real people, or real locales are used fictitiously. Other names, characters, places and incidents are products of the author's imagination, and any resemblance to actual events or locales or persons, living or dead, is entirely coincidental.

Walkabout Publishing
S.D.Studios
P.O.Box 151
Kansasville, WI 53139

© 2007-11 Stephen D. Sullivan

All rights reserved, including the right of reproduction in whole or in part in any form. No part of this publication may be reproduced or transmitted in any form or by any means, electronic or mechanical, including photocopying, recording, scanning, or any information storage and retrieval system, without written permission of the publisher.

Cover art and design by Stephen D. Sullivan.

Proofread by Janet Deaver-Pack. Thanks, Janet!

The Blue Kingdoms™ is the property of Stephen D. Sullivan & Jean Rabe.

Walkabout Publishing logo and other indicated marks in this book, as well as all major characters, are trademarks of Stephen D. Sullivan.

For Steve Winter —
Who always enjoys a good horror yarn.

CONTENTS

THE BLOOD-RED ISLE

FESTIVAL AT WOLFNACHT

THE BLOOD-RED ISLE

I. The Unexpected Jungle

"I thought Isla Sangre was supposed to be a blasted rock," Rik Armstrung said as he stepped ashore. He glanced back at the twelve people disembarking alongside him: nine humans, beside himself—including a derenki—and three basilisks. A rugged crew, for the most part, but the landscape ahead didn't look like what they'd signed aboard for.

"Yeah," the Midknight named Memnon agreed. "This place is as overgrown as the jungles of Kesh."

Lush vegetation tumbled down from the island's mountainous peak all the way to the shoreline. Thick brush and tangled vines sprouted between the crags and boulders lining the water's edge. An aroma of flourishing greenery and slow decay hung in the air. The isle's sweltering humidity smothered every sound, even the lapping of the waves against the shore. Though Rik peered hard into the jungle, he saw no sign of the palace they'd come all this way to find.

Memnon's fellow Midknight, Antiope, giggled—an action ill-suited to a mercenary warrior. Her deep blue armor seemed inappropriate to Rik as well, exposing far too much skin to really protect her. "Are you sure you've got the right island, Baron?" she asked.

"We're sure," Baron Robellar replied. He flashed a cold stare toward both Midknights as he stepped out of the sampan, setting polished boot to rocky shore. "Persha doesn't make mistakes, do you, Persha?"

Persha, Robellar's personal mage, fumbled with her scroll cases and managed a brief smile for her boss. "Of course not, milord. Reifworm and I have followed the trail as faithfully as Al-Shakir follows the stars."

Rik looked from the maroon-robed girl to the captain of Robellar's guard. Al-Shakir was tall, muscular, and obviously very capable; he was also extremely superstitious. Rik wasn't sure whose judgment he trusted less: Persha's, Shakir's, or that of Tel Reifworm, the sea mage who had guided them all to this overgrown rock; none of the three seemed to be sailing with a full crow's nest. Rik trusted Robellar, though—or, at least, he trusted the baron's greed.

"We were lucky to find this isle at all," Reifworm added, getting out of their small boat. Chun Ping, the expedition's captain, tied the sampan's line to a rocky crag, and Reifworm put a binding charm on the rope to hold it in place.

"It's only because of Persha's excellent research that we are here at all," Reifworm continued. "If she hadn't turned up a stone native to Isla Sangre, we'd never have been able to navigate through the warding spells set around the island."

"We are lucky to get here at all," Chun Ping said distantly. "This is not a good place to sail." She gazed longingly toward her junk, moored five hundred yards offshore. The boat's sails hung limp, as though this entire part of the World-Sea was holding its breath.

Persha finished collecting her gear, plopped down on a boulder, and wrung out the soggy hem of her gold-trimmed maroon robe. "The Blood-Red Queen's enchantments have protected Isla Sangre a long time," she said. "Despite her fierce reputation and considerable occult powers, Sanguinarre didn't want people to find her island."

"Nor did the wizards who killed her," Robellar added. "The Mistress of Pain had enemies, but her enemies also have enemies. Keeping the isle secret was good for all of them. And, as it turns out, good for us, too." A smile tugged at the corners of his stern lips as he stared into the jungle, which crowded down the rocky shore nearly into the water. "We all know what we're here for— and it's got nothing to do with the late queen's politics."

Zhek, Brak, and Grif, the company's three basilisk mercenaries, grunted noncommittally. Apparently the lizard-men didn't understand the baron's full motivations any more than Rik did. Robellar *might* want the loot from this isle to secure his position back home, or he might want the fame of having found Sanguinarre's treasure, or he might have some other unfathomable political motivation. But the basilisks, like the Midknights, Rik, and most of the others in the company, were in this purely for the wealth.

"Well, I don't like this place," put in Lita, the baron's paramour. Her golden jewelry rattled as she clung to Robellar, and her blond hair hung damply across her smooth shoulders. She seemed to fear that, at any moment, the jungle itself might attack them.

For once, Rik agreed with the courtesan—even if he couldn't fathom why the baron had brought her along. Dragging around a concubine defied common sense: there would be plenty of time for debauchery after the treasure had been won.

Isla Sangre had been a bad place when Sanguinarre ruled it, and it was still bad. Rik and the rest had come to extract treasure from a lifeless crag, and instead found a jungle. That made Rik feel uneasy, too.

"Tosh!" Wharkun, the derenki, scolded. "It's just a bloody great forest. True, we didn't expect to find it, but it's nothing to be afraid of." He leaned against the long handle of his battle ax and twirled his great, walrus-like moustache in his thick fingers. Wharkun was fatter than most of his cold-bred kind, and already the northern heat was causing big droplets of sweat to bead on his ruddy skin.

"The Company of Lian Fyre created this forest," Persha warned. "I'm sure they didn't do it merely for show."

"Our wizard is right," agreed Al-Shakir. "The battle mage and her people never did anything without a purpose. These tangled trees are a warning for those who would defy the Company's will.

They would make such a jungle truly dangerous, in case the queen's allies returned after the war."

Reifworm scoffed. "Izanti and Carnelian Fyre never expected anyone to return here. All of Sanguinarre's retainers are dead. They died alongside their dread mistress. Without my navigational skills and Persha's research, we'd never have gotten close to these shores—and I am the best sea mage in this part of the World-Sea. I predict that we'll find Isla Sangre pleasantly deserted. Look around—not even a bird in the sky or a crab on the shore." He smiled, showing his crooked teeth.

Rik didn't feel sure that the lack of fauna was a *good* thing. He'd been a pirate and sailed with the Selene navy before turning mercenary, and—in his experience—neither appearances nor advice from hired sea mages could be taken at face value. A glance toward Memnon and Antiope told him that the Midknights didn't trust Reifworm any more than he did.

Baron Robellar made a final check of his weapons and equipment; the rest of the expedition did the same. Despite the unexpected jungle, none in the landing party even considered turning back. "Is everyone ready?" Robellar asked.

"Aye," the others replied, all save the basilisks, who grunted, and Lita who said nothing but appeared pale and worried.

"Let's go, then," Robellar said. "Persha, which way?"

The young mage consulted a rough-cut crystal just small enough to fit in her palm and frowned. "This way, I think," she said, pointing directly upslope. "The charm's portents are vague, though. Something's fouling them up."

Chung Ping spat. "Bad magic. This whole island reeks of it."

"The sooner we find what we're looking for, the sooner we'll get back to your precious ship," Robellar snapped. "Follow me." Taking the direction Persha had indicated, he began hacking his way into the jungle.

Al-Shakir followed behind with Wharkun at his side. Lita came next, sticking as close to the two big men as she could. Rik and Chun Ping followed. Then came the two mages, then the Midknights, and, finally, the basilisks.

The untamed jungle did not easily give way before their machetes. The trees were thick and tangled with underbrush and vines. Rik saw no wildlife as they climbed and cut their way toward the island's central peak. Nor did he see any game trails or other signs that anything lived on the isle.

The canopy remained eerily quiet, aside from the rhythmic hacking of the expedition's blades and the pant of the group's breathing. No insects buzzed through the air or scuttled beneath their feet. The entire world was green, silent, and oppressively hot.

When they stopped to rest, Rik had no clear idea of how much progress they'd made. Their hand-hewn trail seemed to close behind them as soon as they passed. The former pirate couldn't see more than a dozen yards back the way they'd come—nor could he see any farther ahead.

He noticed Chun Ping glancing back downhill, perhaps seeking a glimpse of her anchored junk. She hadn't wanted to come on this voyage, Rik knew, but her mistress in the Sisterhood had commanded it. The pirate queens, it seemed, had an interest in Baron Robellar's fortunes.

Persha sat on a fallen log, consulting her crystal, but apparently didn't like what she saw. Reifworm skulked behind her, as though trying to read over her shoulder. "What do you see?" he asked.

"It's all very hazy," she replied. "I don't understand it. The way to the palace seemed clear during our voyage."

"The bad magic is stronger here," Al-Shakir put in. "Even the stars would not reveal our fates in this place."

Wharkun blew out a long breath. "You got your bloody magic number for the expedition, Al-Shakir" he said. "What more do you want?"

Robellar's giant bodyguard frowned. "Nine is a bad number for treasure hunting," he said. "Twelve is much better."

"Which is why you invited the lizard men," Wharkun said, casting a disdainful glance at the basilisks. "I don't know which smells worse, them or this jungle."

Rather than resting, Zhek, Brak, and Grif took the opportunity to open their smelly rucksacks and eat. Scraps of raw fish dangled from their slavering jaws. One of them, Brak, Rik thought, looked up and said. "Fresh meat always best." As he spoke, fish guts dripped from his sharp teeth.

Lita turned away, looking even more disgusted than Wharkun did. The basilisks took no notice of their comrades' distaste.

Memnon and Antiope sat to one side of the group, whispering to each other. Rik wondered if they, like he, had noticed that the party *actually* numbered thirteen—not twelve, as Al-Shakir claimed. Of course, the bodyguard had probably not included Lita. Rik couldn't blame Robellar's man for that. To Rik, the former pirate, the girl also seemed like baggage.

"Well?" Robellar asked Persha impatiently.

"My crystal isn't working properly," the mage replied, stuffing the rock into her pack. "According to my research, one of the castle's hidden outposts shouldn't be too far ahead."

"If your crystal is faulty, how do you know we're going the right way?" Lita asked.

Reifworm scowled at her. "The palace is at the peak of the island. So long as we head uphill, we'll find it eventually."

The sea mage's answer didn't seem to comfort the concubine. She kept fussing with her hair and trying to wipe the grime off her bare legs. She was dressed even less appropriately than Antiope, though Wharkun didn't seem to mind the way either woman looked. The big derenki ogled both of them whenever he thought no one was watching.

Robellar took a final drink from his waterskin and stood. "You basilisks take point for a while," he commanded.

The lead basilisk, Zhek, grunted his assent. Rik had conversed with the lizard-men several times during their journey to the isle, so he knew they could understand the baron's orders. Now that it came down to business, neither Zhek, nor Brak, nor Grif seemed to have much to say. Rik admired the lizard-men's stolid work ethic.

The basilisks picked up their machetes and began hacking their way uphill. The baron and the others fell in behind.

Lita remained sitting on her log, rubbing her gold-sandaled feet. "You go ahead," she said. "I'll catch up." She wiped the sweat from her brow and muttered to herself.

"Armstrung," Robellar said, "look after her. Make sure she doesn't fall too far behind."

Rik frowned.

"I could stay with the girl if you like, Baron," Wharkun offered.

Robellar eyed the derenki and shook his head. "Armstrung can do it. Can't you, Armstrung?"

"Yeah," Rik replied. He settled back against a tree trunk as the others forged ahead. Only Chun Ping paused long enough to give him a farewell nod. Her glance seemed to say, *"Good luck with your pretty package."*

Rik flashed the pirate captain a pained smile.

When the others had passed nearly out of sight, Rik took Lita by the arm. "Come on, princess," he said, pulling her to her feet. "Time to go."

For a moment, anger flared in the girl's brown eyes. She removed Rik's hand from her arm and began trudging through the undergrowth once more.

They'd barely gone a half-dozen steps, when a strange, hissing cry pierced the jungle's silence.

II. Death Among the Trees

Rik drew his cutlass and sprinted to catch up to the expedition, pulling Lita along with him. She stumbled twice, so he scooped her up over his shoulder and continued running. The courtesan squirmed, but didn't actually protest.

Minutes later, Rik burst through the foliage to find the company stopped in a line along the edge of a narrow chasm. Robellar and the rest peered intently into the fissure.

Rik put the girl down. "What happened?"

"The crevasse just opened up in front of us," Antiope said.

"Tosh!" Wharkun scolded. "This hole's been here for an eternity. Just look at how the vegetation's grown around it!"

"Grown over it," Chun Ping corrected.

Antiope scowled at them both. "How it's grown is not the point, is it?"

"One of the basilisks fell in," Memnon said flatly.

The two remaining lizard-men stood on the edge of the crevasse, peering into the dark shadows below.

"Should we climb down after him?" Lita asked, straightening her silk garments.

Wharkun eyed the girl greedily. "Not bloody likely!"

The basilisk named Grif shook his head. "Zhek lost," he said in his hissing, reptilian voice. "Didn't see pit until too late. Keep moving."

"He's right," Robellar agreed. "There's nothing we can do except be more careful from now on. There will be plenty of time to mourn the dead later."

The speech sounded insincere to Rik, but the others seemed to accept it. For once, the talkative mages had nothing to add.

"This way," Brak rasped, taking the lead.

They moved cautiously to the east until the fissure narrowed to a crack. Then they headed north once more, being careful in

16

case the smothering green vegetation should disguise any more unexpected pitfalls.

If the loss of their fellow saddened Brak and Grif, the basilisks didn't show any signs. They kept hacking through the undergrowth, their powerful muscles cutting a wide path for the rest to follow.

Rik brought up the rear, making sure that Lita didn't fall too far behind.

Soon, the slope steepened, and the expedition was forced to climb. Ascending proved little trouble for the basilisks, the Midknights, or the pirate-trained Chun Ping and Rik. The rest required assistance, especially the mages and Lita. Baron Robellar struggled, too, though he tried not to let it show.

As morning stretched into early afternoon, the heat and humidity intensified. Sweat poured down Rik's face, and his muscles ached as though they might cramp at any moment. Keeping Lita in line was proving more and more troublesome. The generous view he got of her round ass as they climbed didn't lessen his annoyance.

By the time they reached an outcrop large enough for all twelve of them to rest on, even the basilisks seemed exhausted. The group sat together, panting and drinking water. For long minutes, no one spoke.

Finally, Memnon asked, "How much treasure do you think we'll find?"

Rik resisted the urge to roll his eyes. One or the other of the Midknights had started this conversation at least a half-dozen times during the voyage. Did they expect the answer to change?

"There's no way of knowing," Persha replied.

"The wealth should be considerable," Reifworm added. "There are no reports of those who slew Sanguinarre returning with any treasure."

"Some wizards are not interested in gold," Chun Ping said, looking disdainfully at Reifworm.

"Only fools and priests don't want money," Robellar said. "The riches of the Blood-Red Queen were nearly incalculable." He chuckled. "There should be plenty to go around."

"Even after you take your generous share for financing this little expedition," Memnon added.

"I don't think we've much cause to grumble," Wharkun added jovially. "All our shares are somewhat *larger* now." He glanced meaningfully at the basilisks, but if the lizard-men felt offended by the derenki's offhand reference to their dead friend, they didn't show it.

Persha stood, shielded her eyes against the afternoon glare, and gazed upslope.

"What is it?" Lita asked nervously. "What do you see?"

"Ruins, I think," the mage replied. "Not very far off. It's hard to make out through the greenery."

"I will check," Al-Shakir said. "All of you wait here and rest. Even if this is an entrance to the palace of the Blood-Red Queen, we still have a long way to go."

"I'm well rested now," Wharkun said, "and tired of waiting around, sweating." He made to follow.

"Sit down and do as Al-Shakir says," Robellar told him. "I'm paying *him* to make decisions, not you."

Reluctantly, the big derenki plopped himself down on a nearby rock.

Rik tried not to let his disdain for Wharkun's attitude show. Most of Rik's companions seemed entirely too eager to stick their necks out—and it was usually the warrior with his neck farthest out who got his head chopped off. Only Chun Ping seemed to be taking a sensible, mercenary attitude toward this business; all the rest seemed swept up in treasure fever.

A short time later, Al-Shakir returned. "The way ahead is easier," he said, "and the ruins are not far. I cannot tell if they lead to the main part of the castle, though."

"Anything to get out of this accursed jungle, even for a minute!" Lita said. She wiped her hands on the dirty silk of her flimsy outfit.

"Be careful what you wish for," Chun Ping warned.

"I'm with the girl," Memnon said. "I've had enough of this hellish green sweatbox. Sanguinarre and her people are dead and gone, so what are we waiting for? Let's go."

"Armstrung," Robellar commanded, "take the basilisks and help Al-Shakir blaze the trail."

"What about her?" Rik asked, indicating Lita.

"Wharkun can help Lita," the baron replied. "When he's up front, he slows us down anyway."

Rik nodded. Wharkun, rather than being stung by the baron's remark, flashed Rik a secret grin. An old pirate adage about "a pyromaniac tending the powder" leapt to Rik's mind, but he said nothing. He wasn't being paid to make decisions.

The slope ahead flattened out gradually, and Rik, Al-Shakir, and the basilisks made good time cutting their way to the edge of the ruins.

It was difficult to tell whether the tumbledown stone keep had once been an outpost for the queen's guards, or if it was a lower entrance to the palace itself. The ruin's crumbling walls ran upslope, into the jungle, before vanishing into the side of the mountain. Thorny vines crowded the tower's gaping entrance. Beyond the tangled vegetation lay darkness.

"A fine, grand midden," Antiope noted as she and the rest of the group caught up.

"I will enter first, my lord," Al-Shakir said, "to make sure it is safe."

"The living have nothing to fear from the dead," Robellar replied, but his glance told Al-Shakir to proceed.

Persha handed the bodyguard a glowstone, and Al Shakir set it in the golden band around his forehead. Then he hacked through the vines and stepped inside the crumbling tower.

A few moments later, he called back, "I see no danger. There is a passage sloping upward. Perhaps it leads to the palace."

"Good," Robellar said. "Armstrung, you and the basilisks next. The rest of us will follow."

Persha offered Rik a glowstone, but he shook his head; he didn't have a headband to set it in, and he wanted both hands free in case he needed to fight. Grif and Brak pushed through the portal ahead of him, brushing aside the tangled vines. The thorns protruding from the twisted branches did not bother the lizard-men's scaly hides. Rick followed, hacking aside many of the remaining green tendrils.

The interior of the keep was humid and cool. A few tiny shafts of light leaked in from holes high above in the stone walls. The holes and the light from Al-Shakir's glowstone revealed a broad, dark space filled with vines and crumbling interior walls. The place appeared as though it had been deserted for centuries, rather than just a few years.

"Gods of wrath!" Memnon cried from the doorway.

Rik wheeled, his cutlass at the ready.

Memnon stood at the threshold, clutching at his right biceps. A small trickle of blood fell from the Midknight's arm onto the vine-covered floor. "The damned plant stabbed me!"

The baron eyed the long thorns growing from the twisting vines that filled the chamber. He looked annoyed and rumbled, "Be more careful."

"Our lord is right," Al-Shakir said. "The danger is only beginning. All of you would do well to be more wary." He turned and led the group upward, into the darkened tower's interior. The others followed, though Rik paused for a moment beside a tall pile of rubble.

For a moment, he would have sworn he felt the ground tremble. The tremor was as light as a footfall, but Rik didn't think that it was caused by anyone in their group. Spotting nothing unusual, he turned and caught up with the rest.

Walking just ahead of him, Memnon muttered, "'Be more wary.' Pfah!"

"He's not *our* lord," Antiope griped as the baron vanished in the darkness ahead of them.

"Keep moving," Rik urged.

A crumbling stone stairway exited the far side of the chamber. The stair ascended in a straight line, angling—as near as they could tell—toward the mountain top. Mossy vines, looking like decrepit green hair, dangled from the roof of the corridor.

The moss didn't impede their progress, but several times its wispy touch made Wharkun and the Midknights jump. Lita cowered away from the plants, as afraid of the moss as she was of everything else. Robellar paid little attention to his concubine, but Wharkun doted on her, making sure she didn't trip or fall.

The derenki took every opportunity to touch Lita's bare skin, or to "accidentally" brush against her breasts or buttocks while "helping" her. In Rik's estimation, Wharkun was playing a dangerous game. Still, as the derenki himself had pointed out, the fewer that survived this expedition, the larger the shares for the rest.

Light soon streamed from the passage's exit. Beyond the opening lay more of the verdant mountain slope. Clearly the stairway did *not* run all the way to the castle. Rik fought down a pang of disappointment.

The group exited onto an irregular shelf of vine-covered rock, dotted with boulders, about halfway up the mountain. Several hundred feet above, the bare rock of the mountainside protruded from the jungle. Beyond that, more jungle, though Rik thought he could make out a hint of architectural lines and angles amid the foliage.

"Not *more* climbing!" Lita complained. She gasped as the hot afternoon air hit them all like a slap in the face.

"Did you expect this was going to be a picnic, girl?" Chun Ping snapped.

Robellar glared at the pirate captain, but Chun Ping didn't back down. She returned his stare until Al-Shakir stepped between them. Chun backed away to the edge of the shelf, crossed her arms over her chest, and leaned up against one of the boulders.

"A rockslide, do you think?" Persha asked, eying the bare cliff face.

"Undoubtedly," Reifworm replied. "Notice the rocks on the shelf we're standing on are not covered with vines. The slide happened recently, which may work to our advantage." His gray eyes beamed with greedy anticipation.

"How so?" Robellar asked.

"We know the queen had extensive dungeons below the palace," Reifworm said. "A rockslide as large as the one that did this," he indicated the boulders piled up around them, "may have exposed previously hidden recesses of those dungeons."

"Did Sanguinarre hide her wealth in the dungeons?" Wharkun asked.

"The only way to know is to look," Reifworm replied.

"We should climb now," Al-Shakir said. "We want to reach the summit—and the palace—before nightfall."

"Yes," Robellar agreed. "Everyone, make for that cliff. Al-Shakir, you and the basilisks lead the way. Chun Ping, you can bring up the rear."

The pirate captain glared at the baron.

Antiope giggled and whispered to Memnon, "Shit duty for the captain again. You think she'd be used to it!" The two Midknights grinned at Chun Ping; she ignored them.

Rik cast the pirate a sympathetic glance and then climbed upslope ahead of her.

The rockslide had crushed parts of the jungle between the shelf and the exposed slope. This made the going easier, though the ground remained soft and treacherous. Snaking vines constantly threatened to trip up the treasure hunters, and thorns pricked at their exposed skin.

Wharkun carried Lita on his back part of the way, protecting the concubine from the worst scrapes and bruises. She whimpered and muttered under her breath the whole time.

Rik found himself wishing the big man would slip and squash her. From the anger still burning in Chun Ping's eyes, he guessed the pirate felt the same.

A garden of boulders of all shapes and sizes awaited them on the shelf at the end of the climb. Beyond gaped a huge cave-like entrance in the side of the mountain. Enormous vines, some as thick as a man's waist, thrust out of the cave and cascaded down the side of the mountain. To Rick, the vines looked like the grasping fingers of a titanic emerald giant.

"A short break, I think," Robellar announced, sweating. "Then we'll go in."

Wharkun set Lita down on a flat rock and took a drink from his waterskin. The girl rubbed her toes, griping all the while. Al-Shakir, Grif, and Brak loped forward, peering into the cavern's dark interior, scouting the dangers ahead. Rik took a drink and checked his weapons, as did the baron. Persha and Reifworm mopped their faces with the sleeves of their robes and engaged in an animated conversation about the strata in the stone of the cliff face. Chun Ping shook her head and leaned against one of the toppled boulders.

As she did, a loud CRACK! shook the mountainside. The rock behind the pirate captain gave way, and she fell backward, cursing.

Rik reached for her, but, as he did, the crumbled rock beneath his feet gave way, too. In an instant, a huge swath of rubble began sliding down the mountainside.

Lita screamed.

III. The Red Queen's Dungeons

Chun Ping reached for Rik, but he leapt back, trying to save his own life, and grabbed hold of a stout vine at the edge of the slide. The pirate's eyes pleaded with him, but there was nothing Rik could do as she tumbled down the mountainside.

Robellar was shouting something—orders probably—but Rik couldn't make the words out. His blood pounded in his ears and sweat poured down his skin. He gripped the vine with all his might as the rocks beneath him crumbled and crashed down the slope.

The vine gave under his weight. It slipped only a foot, enough to dangle Rik's toes above a torrent of stone. Grunting with pain, the former pirate gritted his teeth and pulled himself up, praying to the gods that the vine would not break as he climbed. He reached a wider branch of the plant and clung there, panting. Only then did he dare glance over his shoulder to look for Chun Ping.

The pirate had been caught in a stony wave. Chun Ping screamed, terrified, as the rockslide carried her toward the beach far below. The stones smashed through the brush, scouring a wide swath down to the muddy jungle floor.

Chun Ping tried to claw her way free, but she remained trapped in the middle of the slide. She reached for branches to pull herself free, but they lay just out of reach. A series of sickening snaps and soggy impacts echoed upslope, detailing the abuse the pirate's trim body was suffering.

Then the slide surged up, cresting, and tossed Chun Ping high into the air. She landed with a bone-rending crunch atop a broken tree. The trunk skewered her. Blood spurted from her mouth and she hung there, like a butterfly pinned to a display, her face a mask of horror.

Rik turned away and concentrated on maintaining his grip on the vine. The ground shuddered for a few more moments, and then the rockslide ceased. In its wake, it left a bare, muddy slope all the way down to the beach, more than a thousand feet below.

"Gods of Wrath and Mercy!" Wharkun exclaimed. He picked himself out of the brush on the far side of the swath and dusted himself off.

"Not much mercy for Chun Ping," Memnon said, coughing and waving dust away from his face.

Antiope got up slowly. "She should have been more careful."

Rik looked around and saw that all the others—even Lita—had survived. Brak and Grif appeared unscathed and unfazed by the ordeal. They and Al-Shakir, who was also unharmed, had been scouting ahead, and thus were farthest away from the collapse. All the rest were battered and scraped to various degrees. The worst injury seemed to be a fist-sized bruise above Persha's left eye.

"How will we get home without Chun Ping?" the mage asked, rubbing her forehead.

"She's not the only one who can sail a boat," Rik called. He secured his grip on the vines and tried not to think about what would happen if he didn't hold on. "A little help here!" Wharkun and Al-Shakir cautiously made their way over to him.

"Don't worry, Baron," Reifworm said. "I imagine that it will be easier to sail away from this island than it was to reach it."

"I hope so," Robellar replied.

Wharkun extended a hand and helped Rik climb back up to the shelf in front of the cavern entrance.

"Lucky break there," the big derenki said.

"Not for Chun Ping," Rik replied, casting a glance toward the dead pirate. He doubted he'd ever forget the look on her face as he snatched away his extended hand. That decision had allowed him to survive but, despite Rik's years of warrior experience, it had been a difficult choice. Of all the people in the company, Chun Ping had been his favorite.

Al-Shakir stared down slope. "Now we are ten," he said, frowning.

Eleven, thought Rick. *Not that it matters.*

"Well, I bloody well hope you're not expecting another of us to jump off this cliff to make you a better magic number, Al-Shakir!" Wharkun rumbled.

The bodyguard shook his head. "Nine is just as bad as ten. Eight would be better."

Wharkun glared at him.

"Losing Chun Ping is tragic," Robellar said calmly, "but we'll compensate her people when we get back."

Antiope rubbed her bruised knees. "So, you'll be paying our heirs, too, if we get killed?" she asked. "You'll be paying the lizard-man's kin?"

Robellar shook his head. "That wasn't our agreement. Full shares for survivors only."

"So why the special treatment for Chun Ping?" Memnon asked.

"My agreement wasn't with her," Robellar replied. "It was with her superiors in the Sisterhood."

That shut the Midknights up. Few in the World-Sea dared to trifle with the Sisterhood.

"I guess they'll be wanting their boat back, then," Wharkun put in.

"When we're finished with it, yes," Robellar said. He peered from the mercenaries to the gaping hole in the mountainside. "Come on." The baron's brown eyes gleamed with anticipation as he drew his longsword and stepped into the darkness.

Persha and Reifworm brought out their glowstones as the rest of the group followed. Al-Shakir hurried to catch up with his employer. Rik peered warily into the gloom.

Beyond the crumbling entryway lay a huge underground chamber. Clearly, the room had once been part of a dungeon complex—small doorways led off of the main chamber into tiny, foul-smelling cells. Rusty cages, iron maidens, charred braziers, and instruments of torture lay scattered around the overgrown floor. The room was roughly circular, and, on its far side, a crumbling stone stairway wound up the wall. Nearer at hand, another stairway spiraled down into deeper darkness. Broken rocks and rubble littered the floor of the dungeon.

Thorny creepers covered everything. Many of the vines were thicker than a warrior's arm, and some were wider than a tree trunk. The vegetation spilled down from above, a cascade of greenery clinging to the walls and the floor. Verdant stems twined through the cages and over the cell doors, which had been wrenched off their hinges. It was as though the terrible vegetation had stormed the room and seized and crushed everything within. Amid the rubble and foliage lay more than a dozen moldering skeletons.

Some of the corpses were twisted in horrible contortions: others lay sprawled with their limbs outstretched, as though they had been struck suddenly from behind. Mottled green creepers wrapped around the bones, as if seeking to replace the long-rotted flesh with new ropey sinews. A stench of decay and death filled the chamber.

The treasure hunters stood just inside the crumbling chamber entrance. No one moved as they all took in the repellant scene.

Finally, Wharkun broke the silence. "Up or down?"

"Please," Lita squeaked, "I don't want to go down!"

Robellar glanced from one ruined stairway to the other. Thick vines half-blocked the way up, but the way down was almost completely clogged. "Why would a queen of Sanguinarre's power hide her treasures deep in the dark?" the baron wondered aloud.

"She wouldn't," Persha agreed. "From what we know, she reveled in her power."

"Indeed. With her island safe from intruders, why would Sanguinarre want to hide her wealth?" Reifworm added. "She would want to keep her baubles close by—just as your . . . *friend* does." He greedily eyed the jewelry dangling from Lita's slender form.

Antiope huffed. "This looks place more like a playroom than a treasury. We won't find any gold here." There was only a trace of irony in the way the Midknight said "playroom."

"Up it is, then," Wharkun concluded. Impatiently flexing his muscles, he trudged to the stairway and began hacking his way up.

"Help him," Robellar ordered, and the rest of the warriors fell in line, working together to cut back the benighted jungle that barred their way. After their long climb, Rik was glad for the chance to limber up his sword arm again. The baron, the mages, and Lita fell in behind as the group gradually made their way upward.

The next chamber they passed through was much like the first: full of cells, implements of torture, and rotting bodies. The next levels after that presented similar grisly scenes. Occasionally, one of the group investigated a cubicle or a side passage as the rest continued upward. Without exception, the cells proved foul beyond comprehension, while the passageways always dead-ended after a short distance—though several corridors looked as though they had continued before the invasion of the choking greenery.

Rik limited his exploration of the side avenues, feeling not only that poking around slowed the group, but also that straying too far from the main path might prove dangerous. As a successful mercenary, Rik prided himself on avoiding unnecessary risks, and the dungeons of Sanguinarre seemed hazardous enough without looking for additional trouble.

He felt vindicated in his opinion when Reifworm returned from a side trip clutching his left hand. Blood poured down the mage's arm and dripped on the mossy floor. "It's nothing," Reifworm said. "I thought I saw some jewelry on one of the corpses in a cell. When I reached to take it, I stabbed my hand on those damnable thorns."

"Wear gloves next time," Memnon remarked. Antiope laughed.

Reifworm glared at the Midknights, but didn't reply. Persha helped her fellow mage bandage his hand.

"Next time," Robellar said, "take one of the knights with you. We need to investigate all avenues in this place, but I don't want my mages getting injured before we reach our goal."

Neither Midknight seemed pleased at this suggestion, but Reifworm grinned broadly.

Late afternoon sunshine, admitted through tiny holes high in the stone walls, shone into the next chamber. The light revealed something surprising about the ever-present vegetation. Though all of the vines they'd seen previously had been vital and green, some in the new room were brown and withered. Rik noticed the change immediately, but chose not to mention it for fear the mages would investigate and further slow the group.

Reifworm and Persha seemed determined to investigate any oddity they came upon—as though the whole decaying palace was some kind of fascinating experiment. To Rik, the dungeons of Sanguinarre remained merely a deadly maze placed between him and his eventual reward.

As the group hacked its way upward, the withering of the vegetation continued until even the aloof wizards noticed it.

Reifworm tugged loose a brown section of vine and crumbled it in his hands. "These have died since the castle's destruction," he noted.

"How can you tell?" Wharkun asked.

"Because they have grown on top of the devastation caused by Sanguinarre's enemies."

"So Izanti and Fyre's vines caused this destruction and then died afterward," Persha said.

"That is the logical conclusion," Reifworm replied.

"At least it will make the cutting easier," Rik noted.

Al-Shakir eyed the dying creepers suspiciously. "Why are the plants dying?" His tone implied concern that the cause might be a threat to his master.

"Perhaps some lingering magic of the queen's," Persha suggested. "Sanguinarre's enchantments stripped the island of life once—or so the legends say."

"But she's *dead*, right?" Memnon asked.

"I daresay," Robellar replied. "If she or any of her people had survived, do you think we'd have gotten this far?"

Wharkun guffawed. "Not bloody likely!"

Baron Robellar's eyes narrowed as he peered around the chamber. The room was much like those they'd seen previously, aside from dead vines and the pale sunlight streaming in from on high. The chamber was broad and roughly circular, with a staircase ascending one side wall and descending the other, back the way they'd come. There were more skeletons here, many covered in tattered crimson rags. *Perhaps they were servants of the queen*, Rik thought, *rather than prisoners or torturers*. Like their dead comrades below, none had escaped the wrath of Carnelian Fyre and her companions.

The baron turned, peering into all the shadowed corners of the room. "Where's Lita?" Robellar hissed.

A cold chill ran down Rik's spine. Where *was* the girl? They'd been so busy hacking through the brush that he hadn't been paying any attention to her. Judging from the surprised looks on the faces of the rest of the group, neither had any of them.

"Well?" Robellar bellowed.

The Midknights shrugged. "She was at the back of the group, last we saw her," Antiope said.

"We were all working hard," Wharkun explained, sweating. "She should have kept up."

"*Should* have?" the baron roared. His face went so red that it appeared he might burst a blood vessel. The nobleman clenched his longsword tightly and glared at Wharkun.

Reifworm looked from the way they'd come to the ascending stairway. He cleared his throat. "The day presses on," he said. "We should not tarry on the girl's account, despite your feelings for her, my lord."

The baron rounded angrily on the sea mage, and Rik read the conflict on Robellar's face. Clearly, the nobleman cared for the girl—he wouldn't have brought her this far if he didn't—but he didn't want to jeopardize the success of the mission, either.

"I will find her, my lord," Al-Shakir volunteered. "The sun is dipping low. You and the others should continue."

"Yes," Robellar said, some of the tension draining from his face. "Find her and then catch up. Take Persha with you, in case you need any magical assistance—and take that fat walrus as well." He glared at Wharkun. "Perhaps the three of you can keep track of a simple girl where *one* of you could not."

Wharkun nodded, apparently feeling he'd gotten off easy, since the baron *had* charged him with taking care of the girl.

Persha appeared nervous and sweaty as she followed the two warriors back into the dungeons. Soon the pale light of her glowstone vanished into the darkness.

Grif and Brak returned to cutting their way up the ascending stairs. Rik and the Midknights joined them, with Reifworm and the Baron bringing up the rear.

Now we are seven, Rik thought. Despite his misgivings about Lita, he hoped she and the others would return. Though he fancied the prospect of a bigger share of the treasure, he knew that the greater the number in the expedition, the greater the chance that each of them would get home alive.

As the warriors cut through the dry vines covering the portal at the top of the stairs, the dungeons gave way to an actual castle corridor. A many-paned window, its red glass shattered and lying on the floor, stood at the far end of the hallway. All of the doors lining the passage had been rent off their hinges. Carpeting with crimson designs lay bunched and curled like monstrous snake skins trampled beneath the intruding vines.

Gruesome sculptures, and occasionally a cage containing a skeleton, filled the regularly spaced niches along the hallways walls. Many of the statues had been toppled or beheaded by the decaying greenery.

Rik and the rest walked quickly through the corridors, continuing upward. They passed kitchens with spitted cadavers and a banquet hall with skeletal dinner guests. Nothing moved; no sounds, save the noise made by the treasure seekers, disturbed the ruined palace's deathly silence.

The Midknights paused at the great table and gawked at the corpses, most of whom were dressed in rotting red and black leather. Cages, filled with the remains of the queen's victims, dangled from iron chains secured to the room's vaulted ceiling. A man's perfectly preserved corpse was pinned to one wall, his mouth gaping in a silent scream. His guts had been opened up and the skin from the wound pulled taut to either side—a grisly canvas bespeaking the Red Queen's dark appetites.

Piles of bones lay in the room's corners; only rusting shackles gave testament to the fact that the heaps had once been human beings. Instruments of torture—apparently for the use of the dinner guests—sat near the grisly piles.

Memnon shook his head. "That blood-red bitch had a strange sense of fun."

"I don't know . . ." Antiope replied. "Some of her equipment looks fairly . . . amusing." She glanced meaningfully toward a cat-o'-nine-tails hanging on the wall and flashed her lover a furtive smile.

Grif stuck his nose over a large silver soup tureen, filled with blackish lumps and sniffed curiously. Brak pushed a corpse aside and picked up a wide silver serving platter. Nothing in the room looked alluring to Rik—not even the silver-and-crystal jewelry of the guests. To him, everything seemed completely ghastly.

"Leave those be," Robellar told the lizard men. "They're too large to carry right now, and there will be better treasures farther on. We can pick up such trifles on the way out, if you like."

He turned and mounted the stairway on the far side of the room. The basilisks put down the silver, and they, the Midknights, and Reifworm followed the baron. Rik paused just long enough to look out one of the room's shattered windows. Below and to the right, he saw the rockslide that had taken Chun Ping's life. Far below that, barely visible through the crushed trees lay the beach and the tethered sampan.

Part of the former pirate wished he were back on that beach right now; another part wished he had never come on this journey at all. Despite having encountered no actual resistance thus far, a mounting feeling of doom filled his gut. He shook off the emotion, strode to the stairs, and quickly caught up with the rest.

"It shouldn't be much farther now," Reifworm said. His eyes gleamed with anticipation. "The legends say that the queen's chamber occupied the highest point in the keep—and we're nearly there."

"How can you be sure?" Memnon asked.

"I peered through one of the shattered windows in the dining room while you were all admiring the . . . decorations," the mage replied. "Only a few floors remain above us. Plus, the queen would want her throne room to be close to the main banquet hall so as to better attend to her guests."

"Or to eat them," Antiope whispered.

"Finally," Reifworm said, ignoring her, "the vines entangling the castle are growing ever more brittle as we ascend. Soon, they will be as dry as dead leaves. I deduce that this is because of the residual effect of the queen's dark magic trying to overcome the jungle-creating spell of Izanti and Carnelian Fyre."

"That's good news for us, right?" Memnon said.

"It certainly makes cutting the vines easier," Reifworm agreed. He stopped in mid-stride and his brow furrowed. "Now that's odd!"

As in the rest of the upper castle, regularly spaced alcoves lined the crumbling hallway ahead of them. Strangely, all of these niches stood empty, save for the intricate web of vines which covered both the recesses and the walls, too. The vines had become much thinner here; most were barely the width of a finger, and nearly all of them appeared dead and brittle.

Reifworm squinted and walked into one of the alcoves, his hand outstretched to touch the brown vines. But as his fingertips brushed the wall, the ceiling of the niche crashed down on top of him, like a dozen hammers striking an anvil.

The sea mage didn't even have time to scream as his body turned into red pulp.

"Gods of Mercy!" Antiope cried. She and the others instinctively backed away from the crimson ooze that had, moments before, been their companion.

Rik's stomach twisted. Was this merely another accident, or was it some kind of sick trap set by the Blood-Red Queen? In either case, the number of their party had suddenly been reduced to *six*.

"Keep back!" Robellar commanded. "Everyone stay away from the niches."

The basilisks and Midknights didn't need the baron's advice any more than Rik did. None of them would venture anywhere near the deadly alcoves. Rik wondered what the sea mage had seen that lured him to his death.

Brak and Grif glanced at each other, and then gazed back the way they'd all come. If the basilisks were thinking about going home, Rik couldn't blame them.

"Keep moving," Robellar ordered. "I won't come this far only to have the prize slip through my fingers. What happened to Reifworm was tragic, but it's not going to stop me now!"

The others walked forward cautiously, scanning the hallway for more hidden dangers. Rik paused long enough to scoop up Reifworm's fallen glowstone and stick it in his pocket. It would be night soon, and the former pirate didn't relish being caught in the queen's palace without any source of illumination.

The group had just turned the corner at the corridor's far end when the lizard-men suddenly stopped.

"What is it?" Robellar asked.

"Hear something," Brak replied. He and Grif turned back the way they'd come and held their saw-toothed swords at the ready.

IV. Sanguinarre's Throne Room

"You're sure you heard something?" Antiope asked, peering around the corner. The Midknight's scanty armor seemed little protection against whatever she and the other treasure hunters might be facing.

Both basilisks nodded, though their lizard-like faces remained impassive.

"And you're positive the noise came from behind us?" Memnon, asked. "This place echoes like a tomb." He and Antiope drew their swords, as did Rik and the baron.

"Yesss," Grif replied.

"Enemy comes from below," Brak agreed.

The baron shuffled to the rear of the group and the warriors arranged themselves in a defensive formation—the basilisks in their heavy turtle-shell armor in front, with the Midknights and Rik in the second rank.

"Keep an eye to aft," Rik told the baron. "We don't want anyone sneaking up on us from behind."

"Yes," Robellar replied, though his eyes warned Rik that the baron didn't like taking orders.

Rik's sea-trained ears soon heard what the basilisks had sensed earlier: something was moving quickly through the ruined palace, racing up the stairs from the banquet hall, heading straight toward them.

The mercenaries stood hidden behind the bend in the corridor, waiting to cut down the first enemy to appear around the corner. Rik tensed, and sweat beaded on his skin. This was the job he'd been hired to do, but avoiding battle was always the best way to stay alive.

A huge, dark shape appeared at the corridor's turn. The lizard-men leapt forward, serrated blades flashing.

"Stop!" bellowed Robellar.

The basilisks stopped, one with his sword leaning heavily against the intruder's raised greatsword, the other with his saw-toothed blade mere inches from the towering man's neck.

It was Al-Shakir, Robellar's bodyguard.

"Warron's beard!" Al-Shakir gasped.

Persha and Lita nearly plowed into him as the big man pulled up short. The two women seemed startled and afraid. All three of the returning expedition members were dirty, bruised, and bloody.

"A little warning, next time," Antiope said, sheathing her twin shortswords.

"You're lucky we didn't kill you!" Memnon added. He wiped a river of sweat from his brow and lowered his broadsword.

Rik and the lizard-men also relaxed.

Barron Robellar sheathed his longsword, rushed forward, and embraced Lita. The concubine appeared greatly relieved to be back in her master's arms. "I'm glad you're safe," he whispered.

"I was lost," Lita sobbed, "but Al-Shakir found me."

The baron dipped his head to Al-Shakir in gratitude; the bodyguard bowed slightly.

"Where's Wharkun?" Rik asked, a chill running down his spine.

"We don't know," Persha replied.

"Two levels down, we thought we heard the girl calling, but we couldn't locate the source," Al-Shakir said. "So we split up to search the side tunnels."

"The whole palace is honeycombed with secret passages," Persha explained. "We didn't notice any earlier in our explorations, but apparently Lita fell through one."

"It was dark, and I couldn't find my way out," the girl said. "I called for help, but no one came. I-I finally groped my way into one of the side corridors and Al-Shakir found me." She tried, unsuccessfully, to wipe the grime off of her smooth legs and her grubby silk clothing.

"The gods must have guided me to her," Al-Shakir said. "She is a very lucky girl. We rejoined Persha shortly afterward. Then the three of us waited, but there came no sign of Wharkun. So we decided to return to my lord's company."

"We called," Persha said. "Shouted our heads off. And I even tried a locating charm—but it was no good. My magic is nearly useless in this place."

"It's the Blood-Red Queen's curse," Al-Shakir added.

Robellar scowled. "These passageways you found, did they lead to the treasury?"

"Whether to the treasury or the throne room or ever deeper into the pit, who can say?" Al-Shakir replied. "They are a maze. Surely only the Blood-Red Queen herself knew their secrets."

"The sun is setting," Robellar noted. "We need to keep moving. The throne room can't be far now." Lita shuddered and clung to him as though she would never let go. Her golden jewelry rattled slightly as she quaked.

"What about Wharkun?" Rik asked, knowing he wouldn't like the answer.

"He can catch up," Robellar replied, turning to go.

"If he doesn't, it's larger shares for the rest of us," Memnon added with a grin.

Rik resisted the urge to lop the Midknight's head off. The former pirate hadn't known the derenki long, just long enough to know he liked Wharkun better than either Midknight.

At least there are more of us now, Rik thought. *Eight if you don't count Lita. That should make Al-Shakir happy.* He didn't believe in the bodyguard's magic numbers, but for survival, nine was better than six.

"What about Reifworm?" Persha asked, looking around for her fellow mage. "Is he scouting ahead?"

"He had . . . an accident," Robellar replied.

"You could say he cut himself out of the take," Memnon added slyly.

"Squashed himself out, is more like it," Antiope put in. "I'm surprised you didn't notice the bloodstain in the last hallway."

Persha staggered as though she'd been struck in the chest. She went pale and nearly backed into one of the vine-filled niches lining the passageway. Rick caught her just in time, and supported her as she regained her bearings.

The young mage buried her face in her hands. "So much knowledge . . . so many years of experience . . . lost forever!"

"The gods often take those who plumb their secrets," Rik said. He intended the homily as a comfort for the young mage, but wasn't sure it came out right.

The Midknights exchanged sardonic glances.

"We'll need your advice more than ever now, Persha," Robellar said, his voice calm and commanding.

"Of-of course," Persha replied. She smudged away her tears with a dirty sleeve. "I-I found something else in the dungeons while I was searching for Lita. I wanted to show it to Reifworm, but. . . ."

She choked back another sob and reached into her robes. With trembling hands, she held out a rough-hewn black crystal. The stone had twelve nearly regular sides and was half again the size of a man's fist. Its center glowed with a faint emerald light.

"What is it?" Robellar asked. "It's like no treasure I've seen before."

"It's some kind of trap!" Lita said fearfully. "I know it is!" She buried her head on the baron's shoulder.

"I believe it may have something to do with the spell that destroyed the castle," Persha told them. "Its aura is similar to the enchantment I sense in the vines and the destroyed walls."

"A spell?" Memnon asked. "How do you use it?"

The young mage shook her head. "I don't know. It seems incomplete, somehow. Perhaps it was part of a greater enchantment, but it malfunctioned. Lian Fyre was the best battle mage of our era, and Izanti is even more powerful still. Their magics are beyond anything I can fathom."

"Guess, then," Robellar commanded.

Persha screwed up her face in concentration. "Perhaps shattering it...?" she suggested.

"So it's a grenade," Rik said. "Like a fireball gem."

"It could be," Persha replied, "though obviously much more powerful—at least, in the right hands. Whatever it is, I hope we won't need it. It could be very dangerous. Besides, other than ourselves, we still haven't seen any living thing in the palace. We should be relatively safe."

"Lack of enemies hasn't stopped people getting killed," Antiope observed.

Persha took a deep breath. "Yes, but largely through their own carelessness," she said.

"Poking his nose where it didn't belong is what got Reifworm squashed," Memnon said.

"That's why we should be doubly cautious—especially with an enchanted object like this," Persha said. She gazed at the baron. "We should take this home and study it—unlock its secrets. Think of the advantage a weapon designed by Izanti or Lian Fyre could give your armies, Milord."

Robellar extended his hand. "Give it here."

Persha handed him the stone, and he stowed it in a large leather pouch hanging from his belt. "Be careful with it, my baron," she warned. "I can't stress enough how dangerous it might be."

"Everything in this accursed place is dangerous," Robellar replied.

"Including us," Memnon boasted. Grif and Brak hissed in agreement.

"Come on," the baron said. "Time's wasting."

The light continued to wane as they trekked through the deserted, vine-covered corridors and up a winding stairway to the next level of the palace.

The stairway debouched into one end of a long, wide hallway; another stairway, even more clogged with vines, descended from the corridor's far side.

On one side of the hall—the south, Rik judged by the failing light—stood a great bank of windows, stretching from floor to ceiling, twenty feet overhead. The vines covering the room's walls and floors had shattered the windows' panes of glass, though the opening's crosspieces remained intact. Broken red glass formed a mosaic of shards amid the dry flora blanketing the floor.

Moldering red and black curtains bracketed the window casements, but no breeze disturbed the draperies. Ornate furniture—gilded chairs, couches, and tables, all smashed to pieces by the invading vegetation—lay scattered around the room. Dusty tapestries, some more than fifty feet long, covered the wall opposite the windows. The hangings depicted the most depraved warfare and torture—hideous practices clearly sanctioned by the Blood-Red Queen. Fortunately, so far as Rik was concerned, the invasive vines obscured many of the hangings' more grisly details.

"I may not know art," Antiope joked, "but I know what I like."

"Shut up!" barked Robellar. Clearly, the atmosphere of the palace was finally unnerving him.

In the middle of the tapestries stood a huge pair of gilded doors, leaning askew on their broken golden hinges. Withered vines, like a great russet tide, spilled out of the doorway into the room beyond. A creeper the size of a tree trunk ran between the doors and out the window opposite before snaking down the side of the keep.

"We've found it!" Memnon gasped. "Those have to be the doors to Sanguinarre's throne room!"

Rik wasn't listening to the Midknight. Something about the vines in this room had caught the former pirate's attention.

41

Cautiously, Rik crossed to the tapestry wall to get a better look. Where previously the vines had been verdant green or withered brown, some of these appeared almost . . . red. What's more, as he stared at them, Rik could almost swear they moved—pulsing softly in the fading daylight.

He blinked and rubbed his eyes. Could it have been a glimpse of the pulsing vines that lured Reifworm to his grisly death? Or was the movement merely a figment Rik's overworked imagination? He reached out to touch one of the red creepers and then stopped, remembering Reifworm's fate.

Crash! Both of the big doors smashed to the floor as the Midknights and the basilisks pulled the golden gates down to gain better access to the room beyond. The doors' impact sent clouds of gray and brown dust into the still air. The crimson glass on the floor shivered.

The mercenaries, the mage, and the baron gasped in wonderment. Rik rejoined the group at the portal's threshold and stared into the room beyond.

The queen's chamber was enormous, easily twenty five yards wide and twice that long—so long, in fact, that in the failing light, it was difficult to make out the far reaches of it. The hall's gilded walls rose thirty feet before arching into a great dome. A bank of graceful windows, curved outward like the edges of a scallop shell, dominated the far wall. Before the magical vines had ruined them, the windows must have been spectacular; now their empty oval panes looked like pale eyes, staring across the shadowed ruins.

The glowlight in Persha's hand flared and pushed back the darkness, and the entire room glittered. There was gold everywhere: tables, chairs, divans, grotesque statuary, the obscene friezes carved into the walls, barbed scrollwork and decorations— all shone from beneath a thick layer of brown and crimson vines.

Rik didn't have time to figure out whether the furniture was solid gold or merely gilded before something more caught his eye—*jewels*. Thousands of glittering gemstones lay amid the decaying vegetation. Rubies, emeralds, diamonds, sapphires all glimmered in the glowstone's light. Some of the gems were set in the room's shattered furniture, others were part of abhorrent mosaics, and still more were fitted into the jewelry wound around the bodies of the room's many skeletons.

Nearly two dozen corpses littered the chamber's vine-strewn floor. These were not the bodies of servants, or guests, or victims like those they'd seen in other parts of the ruins; these were Sanguinarre's prized guards, courtiers, and devotees. The bracelets entwining their limbs, the diadems circling their foreheads, the jeweled girdles around their bony waists, and the glittering curved daggers at their hips all spoke of the Red Queen's favor.

Rik looked at Lita, hugged close to the baron. Her jewelry, too, glimmered. The girl clutched nervously at the ruby pendant dangling from her throat.

These people were like her, Rik thought. *They were courtesans devoted to the queen—and their devotion got them killed.* He silently vowed never to get killed for an employer, especially not Robellar.

A sudden shout shattered the silent tableau.

"Now *this* is what I signed on for!" Memnon said, grinning. He sheathed his sword, put his hands on a stout vine, and vaulted across the throne room's threshold. "That's a lot of loot for seven people!"

Eight, counting Lita, Rik thought.

Memnon stooped and began pulling a bejeweled arm band from the nearest corpse. As he did, a sudden swirl of wind filled the room. Red dust rose from the floor and shaped itself into a monstrous visage. The face was huge, taller than a man, with burning red eyes, pointed ears, and curving horns atop its head. The fact that the thing was transparent didn't make it any less terrifying.

Antiope shrieked.

43

Memnon stood, startled, and dropped the arm band. Before he could react, the frightening apparition rushed across the room and hit him full in the chest.

The demon-headed specter knocked Memnon from his feet and pushed him back, across the room and out the doorway. Rik reached for the Midknight as he shot past, but, as with Chun Ping, Rik's attempt to save his fellow mercenary came too late.

Everyone watched in horror as Memnon crashed out the antechamber windows, shattering the skeletal mullions. The red and black curtains next to the windows billowed outward with the rush of the Midknight's passing. The demon head went with him, vanishing like mist on a summer afternoon as Memnon plummeted from its grip. The Midknight screamed as he fell—a high-pitched, terrified wail that ended with crushing suddenness.

Rik and Al-Shakir rushed to the window and peered out. Two bloody smears on the castle walls indicated the route of Memnon's departure. The Midknight's broken body lay almost directly below them, on the shattered cliff at the top of the rockslide which had claimed Chun Ping. Beyond the Midknight, Rik could still make out the tree-impaled corpse of the pirate captain, a black silhouette against the darkening jungle.

Back in the anteroom, everyone else had frozen as Memnon and the specter rushed past. Antiope quaked uncontrollably. Robellar shook as well, and even the basilisks seemed paralyzed.

"It's just a spell!" Persha whispered, almost pleading. "We've nothing more to fear. It's just a demonhead spell—some form of residual magic. It's spent now. We've nothing more to fear!"

"Nothing to fear!" Antiope shrieked. "You silly little bitch! That hex just killed my man!" She lunged across the space separating them and slapped the mage across the face, hard.

Persha staggered back. Antiope strode forward to hit her again, but Brak stepped between them.

"You want to fight, lizard?" the Midknight asked, drawing her twin shortswords.

Grif stepped up next to Brak, though neither of them replied to Antiope's taunt. Both basilisks held their saw-toothed swords at the ready.

"Well, sod you," Antiope said. "Sod you both! You're not worth killing."

"Enough!" barked Robellar. "Memnon's death is tragic, but we've reached our goal! We've found what we came for. I'll kill both you and the basilisks before I let you ruin this, Midknight." He took a step toward the throne room and motioned for the rest to follow.

"You first," Antiope hissed, her eyes full of hatred and anger.

Al-Shakir pushed past his boss. Hefting his big oval shield and greatsword, the bodyguard climbed over the vines into the wreckage-strewn chamber. When no new sorcery rushed up to kill Robellar's man, the rest of the group clambered into the throne room behind him.

They spread out near the door, searching the corpses, prying free the spectacular jewelry. The basilisks gnawed through the limbs of the skeletons to obtain their prizes. Antiope's lust for gold soon quelled her recriminations over the death of her lover.

"Find the crown jewels," Robellar ordered. "They'll be worth more than all the rest combined."

Rik stood, fastening a ruby and pearl bracer around his left wrist. "If the queen's corpse is here," he said, "it should be near her throne. I'm guessing that would be the big golden chair on the far side of the room." He grinned. Now that they'd won their treasure, the perils of the journey didn't seem so bad.

Robellar kicked aside the corpse he'd been picking over; Lita shuddered and gritted her teeth. "Of course," the baron said. "Good thinking, Armstrung. Remind me to offer you a captaincy once we get home."

As if I'd take it, Rik thought. He gave the nobleman a curt bow and smiled sincerely.

Just then, the setting sun dipped below the horizon, and the sky beyond the far windows turned brilliant crimson. The silhouetted throne loomed large in the blood-red light, as if beckoning the fortune hunters. The group moved quickly toward it, Robellar and Lita in the lead, each member of the group excited by the prospect of even more spectacular treasure.

As the explorers walked, the withered vines tugged at their legs, and the bejeweled corpses shifted slightly on the floor.

Persha cried out, and they all turned as she pulled a long thorn from her ankle. The blood dripping from the spike glistened like rubies in the sunset illumination. "It's nothing," the mage said, "I—!" Then her eyes went wide, and she screamed.

The others whirled, following her stare. A body dangled upside-down in an alcove on the far side of the room: Wharkun—their missing comrade. In the dimly lit room, none of them had noticed the big derenki. His blue eyes stared blankly at the floor; his throat had been cut from ear to ear. Red, pulsing vines wrapped around his corpse, as though they were feasting on the dead warrior's blood.

"Gods of Mercy!" Antiope gasped.

"How in the name of the Seven Hells did he get here?" Robellar asked.

"I brought him here," Lita said. "Just as I brought the rest of you."

"Wha—?" Robellar began, turning toward his paramour. As he did, Lita plunged a jeweled dagger into his chest.

V. The Blood-Red Queen

The baron gazed down at the weapon protruding from his breast, his face a mask of shock and horror.

"Sorry, 'my love,'" the girl purred. "But this is the *real* reason I came with you."

"W-why?" Robellar gasped.

"To serve my queen," Lita replied. "I wasn't here when they slew her, so I'm the only one left. I am *Kellita* of Isla Sangre— acolyte of the Mistress of Pain and the last of my kind. The enchantment surrounding the island kept me from returning on my own. Now, thanks to you and this company of fools, I am home, and Sanguinarre will rise again!"

She let go of Robellar and he slumped to the floor, his blood seeping into the pulsing red vines at her feet.

Al-Shakir screamed, "No!" and leaped toward the girl. As he did, the blood-red creepers sprang to life. They whipped up off the floor and twined themselves around the bodyguard's arms and legs, suspending him in the air like a fly caught in a web.

Kellita pulled the dagger from Robellar's body and cut Al-Shakir's throat. The big man gasped and his hands jerked open reflexively. His weapons and shield clattered to the floor, useless.

As Al-Shakir died, the vine-tangled corpses of Sanguinarre's dead servants rose to their feet.

"Teats of Kabree!" Antiope cried, barely lifting her twin swords in time to fend off a skeletal claw.

Kellita laughed and gestured toward the rest of the warriors, directing the hideous, undead army to attack.

Rik and the basilisks sprang to action, hacking at the limbs of the nearest corpses, while, at the same time, yanking their own feet free from the entangling vines. Rik glanced toward the doorway, hoping to make a speedy exit, but animated skeletons and a sea of writhing vines blocked his way.

"Fingall's balls!" he muttered under his breath.

Persha shrieked and backed toward the left-hand wall of the room, stabbing at the ropy tendrils with her dagger as she went. The vines kept reaching for her, like a wave of striking snakes.

"Ironic, isn't it?" Kellita said, chuckling. "You thought you were dragging me into this place, when all the time, I was leading you." No longer was she the baron's tremulous concubine; now she was reveling in her power as a high priestess of the sadistic queen.

"Persha would never have found that stone from the isle if I hadn't secretly led her to it. Nor would that fool Reifworm have been able to sail us through the island's protective spells without my subtle prodding. I even slipped away from the rest of you long enough to lure Wharkun through a secret passage to kill him. I did all of it just to arrive at this moment. Now your blood will bring my queen back from the pit. She shall rise again, and I will rule at her side."

She stooped and seized Robellar's corpse under the arms. She cut the baron free from the writhing vines and pulled him toward Sanguinarre's golden throne.

The rough handling of her lord's dead body seemed to snap the grip of fear paralyzing Persha. Her back against the wall, she gestured in an arc and muttered a quick incantation. In response, a two-foot-tall wall of blue-white flames sprang up around her. The tendril vines attacking the mage withered and reeled back, green serpents recoiling from fire. Larger, stouter vines began creeping forward to take their place.

Rik, the two basilisks, and Antiope were fighting nearly side by side, but most of the forces of the dead queen were arrayed between them and the doorway.

"If we can't go out," Rik said, "we'll have to go in." He fastened his eyes upon Kellita, who had dumped the baron's corpse by the throne and was now chanting over the body.

"Right," Antiope agreed. "That bitch is the weakest part of her own scheme. If we take her down, we can still walk out of here rich."

Walking out *at all* was Rik's main concern, but if he could escape wealthy—why not?

"Yesss," Brak grunted. He and Grif surged toward the dangling body of Al-Shakir, between them and Sanguinarre's acolyte. Rik and Antiope followed, protecting the group's rear. Of the thirty or so zombies originally facing the mercenaries, a scant dozen remained. The rest they'd hacked into so many pieces that all the vines in the world would not be able to stitch the undead back together.

Those dozen remained fanatical and deadly foes. Feeling neither pain nor fear, the reanimated corpses rushed after the mercenaries. Only the entangling vines covering the floor and the zombies' puppet-like awkwardness kept the undead from overwhelming the four warriors remaining.

In the corner, Persha's firewall was quickly fading, but she had conjured a new type of magical protection around herself. The magical shield flashed with blue-white energy every time a vine tendril tried to attack her. The tendrils withered and died, but the spell seemed to be taking all of Persha's concentration.

Rik and the others reached Al-Shakir's body, near where Robellar had fallen. Kellita stood two dozen yards away, her arms raised in supplication as she chanted dark supplications to her dead queen. The acolyte was facing away from mercenaries, but an ocean of writhing vines lay between the warriors and the wicked concubine. Beyond Lita, something large began to push the mass of vines upward.

As Rik, Grif, and Antiope fought off the animated corpses, Brak stooped and retrieved Al-Shakir's fallen spear. The basilisk hefted the weapon and took careful aim. Then he hurled the spear at Kellita's smooth back.

At the last second, Sanguinarre's priestess turned. The spear skidded over her left shoulder blade and sliced through one of the bejeweled straps crossing her back. Part of Kellita's gossamer clothing fluttered to the floor. Hatred blazed in the girl's eyes.

"*Nebet rahsan sengat!*" she hissed. She stretched out her hands and a searing crimson ball of ectoplasm shot across the room.

The hex struck Brak full in the chest, lifting him off his feet and propelling him across the chamber. His turtle shell armor sizzled as the lizard-man soared out the window and disappeared over the wall, just as Memnon had. Unlike the Midknight, Brak did not scream.

Roaring a curse in the tongue of his people, Grif charged forward. He bowled over two skeletons in his way, shattering their bones like twigs, and cut down a half-dozen vines as wide as a man's arm.

Kellita seemed exhausted from her sorcery and, for a moment, Rik dared to hope that the basilisk might actually reach the girl and slay her. Grif raised his saw-toothed sword high.

As he did, a thick vine shot up from the foliage on the floor. Its thorny tip pierced the tortoise shell armor covering Grif's back and burst out his chest in a spray of deep crimson gore. The lizard-man gave a surprised hiss, and the breath rattled out of his lungs for the last time.

"Thank you," Kellita said, licking a droplet of Grif's blood from her lips. "My mistress needed more blood." Her eyes blazed red as she turned toward Rik and Antiope, the last mercenaries standing. Behind the wicked acolyte, the vine-covered shape near the throne shuddered and surged up a few more inches.

Kellita began chanting and a pale red glow built up around her hands. "*Nebet nebet sihir . . .*"

"Do something!" Antiope hissed, her twin short swords felling another vine-encrusted skeleton.

Rik hacked off the arm of the zombie attacking him, whirled, and in a single motion grabbed and threw the dagger at his belt.

The blade soared straight for Kellita's face, but she stopped her chant and said, *"Sildo."* The red magic around her left hand flashed, deflecting the dagger. Before the weapon hit the ground, a burst of white light blazed across the room and struck the acolyte's right shoulder.

Kellita grunted and fell to her knees, bleeding. Her eyes blazed with hatred. "Persha!" she hissed.

Robellar's mage was walking slowly toward the throne, her glowing shield forcing back the writhing crimson vines.

"I thought to save you for last," Kellita said, rising to her feet once more. "Your blood will be powerful—just the thing my mistress needs. Unfortunately, I see that I shall have to deal with you now." She clutched her wounded shoulder and red energy glowed where the blood dripped.

"Pinu!" Persha said, and another burst of sharp white magic blazed from her outstretched hand.

"Sildo!" the acolyte countered, and Persha's knife-like hex sizzled into nothingness.

"If you have another dagger," Antiope whispered to Rik, "now would be a good time to skewer Lita with it." She hacked off the arm of one of the seven corpses still fighting against them.

"Busy now," Rik replied. He stepped away from a skeletal claw and tripped on a vine trying to twine itself around his ankle. He slashed down with his cutlass, severing the stem, and rolled to his left as another creeper tried to grab him.

The vine missed, but something hard dug into Rik's side. Looking down, he recognized the large leather pouch from Baron Robellar's belt. Scooping it up, he thrust the bag into his own belt and brought his sword around just in time to slice through a vine looping around his throat.

A dozen yards away, Persha and Kellita were advancing slowly toward one another. White and red bursts of energy streaked back and forth between the two women, only to be deflected by magical shields. Sweat beaded on their foreheads as they tried to destroy each other.

"Ironic, isn't it," Kellita said, "me turning the enemy's magic to my queen's purposes? Izanti's vines become my mistress' veins and sinews. The blood of those who plotted to steal her treasure becomes her blood."

"Fry in hell, you bitch!" Persha said, sending a cascade of fiery daggers blazing toward her enemy.

Kellita staggered, and, for a moment, Persha smiled. But she didn't see the vines looming up like serpents behind her.

"Persha! Look out!" Rik cried, a moment too late.

Before the mage could turn and reinforce her defense, a huge mass of vines simultaneously thrust themselves into the rear of Persha's magical shield. Some of the tendrils bounced off or sizzled into nothingness, but many forced their way past the enchantment. They seized Persha by the wrists and ankles and pulled. The mage screamed as the crimson vegetation tore her apart, splattering the room with her blood.

As the echo of Persha's final cry faded, the vines behind Kellita peeled away, and the body of the Blood-Red Queen rose from the throne room floor.

The corpse was tall, nearly gigantic, with moldering bones and rotting flesh showing through the gaps in her decaying silken garments. Twisted vines made up her sinews, and scarlet creepers formed her veins. The fibrous vessels lacing across her body pulsed with blood stolen from the queen's latest victims. Golden bracers, gem-encrusted armbands, serpentine anklets, and other priceless ornaments decorated Sanguinarre's putrefying body. A golden girdle carved with obscene and sadistic figures girded her waist. Her jewelry rattled and her sinews hissed and creaked as she moved. Atop her skeletal head a ruby diadem glittered, and in the monster's empty eye sockets burned blazing red eyes.

Kellita fell to her knees and raised her arms in jubilation. "My Queen! You arise! You are nearly complete!" She began chanting once more.

"Sod *me*!" Rik whispered.

"Happily—assuming we live through this," Antiope replied. In her eyes, he saw the mercenary gleam she'd lost when Memnon died. All the corpses fighting against them had stopped moving, and the deadly vines had gone limp as the monster queen drew their power into herself.

"Do you think we can run?" Antiope asked.

"Where to?" Rik replied.

The Midknight nodded grimly. "Ride me to hell and back if we don't have to be heroes," she said. "I'll go left, you go right. Maybe between the two of us we can slag that twisted little bitch and stop the conjuring."

Rik agreed, and the two of them split off, angling for opposite sides of the room. Even immobile, the twisted sea of vines proved difficult to traverse. The dangling vegetation provided cover, and Rik thanked the gods for that. He raced through the concealing foliage until he finally came in sight of Kellita and her dark mistress once more.

The acolyte was so intent on her revivified queen, that it seemed she had completely forgotten the two surviving mercenaries. As Rik emerged from behind a thicket of vines, the evil girl remained kneeling, arms upstretched, a dozen feet away from the rising monster.

The thing that had once been Sanguinarre swayed in front of Kellita, like a serpent before a snake charmer. The girl's enchantment was building: every moment, more of the vines in the room withered and died. And every moment the corpselike Mistress of Pain appeared more human.

Rik spotted Antiope, crouched amid the hanging vines on the acolyte's opposite side.

Stephen D. Sullivan

"Now!" the Midknight cried, springing forward. Instantly, Rik also leapt toward Lita.

Kellita whirled, deadly sorcery on her lips. Antiope drove her right shortsword into the acolyte's side.

"I think I liked you better when you only whimpered, bitch!" the Midknight said. She reeled back with her other sword, aiming at the girl's neck. "This is for Memnon!"

The acolyte pointed, and white-hot flames blazed from her left hand. The hex burned away the right half of Antiope's face, and the Midknight crashed to the ground, dead.

Rik wrapped his arm around Kellita's slender neck and drove his remaining dagger into her back, puncturing her lung and seeking her heart.

The girl whirled and her left hand struck Rik on the side of the head with surprising strength. He stumbled back, his face burning where she'd hit him.

Kellita staggered and fell on all fours, blood gushing from her mouth, gore dripping from the wounds in her side and back. Rik drew his cutlass to finish her.

"Sanguinarre! Save me!" the girl gasped.

Suddenly, the whole floor exploded upward. The crumbling vines disintegrated into dust, and the remaining zombies shattered into shards of bone and splatters or rotted flesh.

The impact hurled Rik across the room. He landed by the doorway, crashing hard onto his back. For a moment, the whole world swirled with flashes of light and darkness.

As Rik's vision cleared, he saw Kellita crawling toward the towering form of Sanguinarre.

"Take me!" the dying girl pleaded. "May my blood be . . . enough. . ."

The titanic corpse queen lifted her bleeding acolyte overhead and tore the girl in two. Kellita's blood rained down hot and crimson on Sanguinarre's twisted flesh. And, as the blood covered

54

her, the decaying body of the Mistress of Pain began to glow bright red.

A terrible laughing sound built within the chamber, a kind of laughter that Rik had never heard before—a sound that came straight from the darkest pits, the sound of the Blood-Red Queen crawling out of the abyss to plague the World-Sea once more.

Outside, black clouds covered the twilit sky and lighting crashed. Thunder shook the palace to its core, momentarily drowning out the terrible laughter. The clouds opened and torrents of rain poured down. A gust of wind sent enormous droplets hissing into the throne room. The hot rain splattered against the blood drenched corpse of Sanguinarre.

Rik staggered to his feet, knowing it was too late to do anything. Even in death, Kellita had won; her monster queen was returning to the world, and nothing Rik could do would stop it. His only hope now was to escape.

He stumbled toward the exit, his body bruised and sore, cuts tracing almost every exposed inch of his skin. His right side ached with every breath he took; he was certain his ribs were broken.

The vines' demise had left his escape route blessedly free from obstacles, but Rik still had trouble putting one foot in front of the other. He wobbled into the antechamber and leaned against the sill of the broken windows.

He looked down the hallway toward the stairs. How would he ever get back to the beach before the Mistress of Pain turned him into the first victim in her new reign of terror? He surveyed the hall's shattered furniture and his gaze settled on the obscene tapestries on the opposite wall. A desperate plan formed in Rik's mind.

The former pirate seized the largest and sturdiest tabletop he could carry and tossed it out of the window. The table sailed over the wall and bounced once off the mountain, before disappearing into the darkness. A flash of lightning revealed it, more or less intact, lying in the mud at the apex of the rockslide.

Inside the throne room, the red glow grew brighter and the queen's laughter louder. The total resurrection of Sanguinarre was very close.

Rik tore the largest tapestry he could find from the wall. Dragging it to the window, he stabbed his cutlass through the hem with all his strength. The sword plunged deep into the hard wood of the windowsill, securing one end of the cloth in place.

He heaved the other end over the side and grinned when it stretched from the heights of the palace to the mountainside below. This plan might work after all! The former pirate tested the windowsill connection for strength and then threw his leg over the rail.

As he tried to hike himself over the sill and out, part of Rik's outfit caught on a broken mullion: Robellar's bag. Something in the pouch pressed hard against Rik's side, making spots dance before his eyes. What was in the bag? Rik's fevered brain could hardly remember—though he thought it might be important.

"You don't have much time!" he muttered to himself, but his fingers opened the bag as if of their own accord. Inside was the glowing stone that Persha had found—poor, dead Persha. What was it she'd said about the stone? It contained magic—the magic of Lian Fyre and Izanti.

Rik glanced from the stone to the throne room and made another desperate choice.

"Chew on this, you twisted red bitch!" he called, throwing the stone into the chamber with all his might.

Then he hurled himself outside, clinging to the tapestry, sliding down into the darkness. Just as he crashed onto the muddy mountainside, a blinding flash of green illumination burst from the ruined castle above him.

Not daring to look back, he half ran, half stumbled downhill until he reached the top of the rockslide. As he'd hoped, the rain had turned the slope below into a mud river.

He jumped face-down on the tabletop, landing on it as though it were a sled, and threw himself over the precipice. Behind him, the castle exploded in another flash of brilliant emerald light.

The whole island shook as Rik hurtled down through the jungle. Lightning crashed and he saw Chun Ping's body, still impaled on the broken tree stump. Then she was gone, and the wet leaves of the jungle were slapping his face once more.

Twice the makeshift sled nearly bucked him off. The former pirate held tight, though both jolts nearly ripped his arms from their sockets.

He landed in a muddy tumble on the rocky beach where they'd left their landing boat moored. Rik looked around; the sampan was gone!

He cast his eyes desperately across the bay. Chun Ping's junk still lay at anchor, unaware that its mistress would never return. And near it, silhouetted against the waves, bobbed the sampan.

Rik looked back. The entire top of the mountain roiled with green flames. Lightning crashed and thunder shook the island. Between the deafening peals, Rik heard the dying wail of the nearly resurrected queen of Isla Sangre.

The green fire burst out of the castle and billowed down the mountain toward shore.

Rik dived into the water and swam.

He was almost half way to the ship when the concussion from the magic hit. The sea rose up and dashed him into the deep, sucking him under with powerful watery hands. The sea crushed the air from his lungs. He tried to swim, but he didn't know which way was up.

A flash of lightning revealed the green eddies surrounding him: green above, green below, green to either side. Desperately, Rik kicked his legs, hoping his body's natural buoyancy would carry him to the surface.

His air ran out before he got there. The world swirled and went dark. Then something jerked him upward.

He found himself in the open air, lying on a hard and wet surface, gasping for breath. Above him loomed a reptilian face that not even a mother could love.

Rik sat up quickly; his head pounded as though someone had struck it. He squinted into the darkness and said, "Brak?"

"Yesss," the basilisk hissed. Somehow, Brak had survived his plunge through the palace window.

Well, Rik himself had a similar fall, so why not? Brak hadn't had a tapestry to help him, but then, Rik didn't have the lizard-man's naturally thick hide and stout bones.

"Thank you for pulling me out of the surf," Rik said.

Brak nodded.

The two of them were in the sampan, the former pirate realized. The basilisk must have taken the small boat from shore, thinking the rest of his companions dead. Brak had very nearly been right.

"Where's the ship?" Rik asked. "Where's Chun Ping's junk?"

Brak pointed to the ocean nearby. Only a mast and a few tattered sheets remained above the waves. Apparently, the blast from the green magic had swamped the larger ship while the much smaller sampan rode out the turbulence.

Rik gazed back toward the island. In a flash of lightning, he saw the jungle, green and verdant, running from summit down to shore. Not a trace of Sanguinarre's palace remained.

The former pirate shook his head. He'd risked life and limb and lost close to a dozen comrades, and all he had to show for it was a gold and pearl arm band. He turned from the island and gazed out to sea. In the west, the storm was abating, and the moon's rings were just peeking above the horizon.

"It's a long way home," Rik said, mostly to himself.

"Yesss," Brak agreed. "'Specially without supplies."

The basilisk looked at Rik and grinned, showing row upon row of knife-sharp teeth. "Fresh meat always best."

FESTIVAL AT WOLFNACHT

I. Intruders at the Gate

Konstantine crept up the stairway and peered over the spikes topping the wooden palisade. Falling snow made the nighttime countryside around Wolfnacht a blur of gray and white. The young villager could barely see the Timberline Mountains—though their peaks loomed just beyond the forest trail. He wiped several large, wet flakes from his eyebrows and stared into the gloom. He'd heard a sound, but what was it? What kind of man or beast would be out on a frigid night like this?

Normally, the village guard would have investigated such noises, but Wolfnacht's guard posts remained empty, and snow covered the catwalks atop the surrounding wall; no one patrolled the palisade tonight.

The sentries are all safe in their homes, Konstantine thought. *Or maybe they're busy with the town elders.* The adults were always busy nowadays, and, as usual, they hadn't seen fit to tell "Stan" what they were up to. Konstantine fumed about that. He was fifteen, and nearly in his majority, but no one had seen fit to tell him the purpose of all the hushed meetings.

Melting snow dripped down Stan's hair and splashed into his eyes. He pushed the sopping black locks away from his forehead. "Fool!" he muttered quietly to himself as he continued peering into the storm. "If you had any sense you'd be inside with all the rest!"

But, despite the wet and the cold, he didn't want to go back inside. There was something about the storm that had compelled him to venture into the night, something he'd felt even before he'd heard the muffled chimes.

This blizzard was *different*. Something about it was making the coarse hair on the back of Stan's neck stand on end. If he could figure out what, then he could go back inside where it was safe and warm.

He heard the noise again—a tinkling, bell-like tone, cutting through the hissing of the wind.

A flash of movement drew Stan's eyes to Wolfnacht Pass, barely visible through the snow. Dark shapes lurked at the base of the mountains, trudging away from the rocky cleft, heading toward the city. Konstantine strained his eyes, but he couldn't make out what the shapes were. He turned toward the alarm bell, dangling from a scaffold on the parapet a dozen yards away. Should he ring it?

No, he thought. *No sense stirring things up. Not on a night like this with everyone so busy. Those shadows could be just a trick of the light and the snow. We're not expecting visitors. And, besides, no one ever comes to Wolfnacht anymore—not unless there's a festival.*

The idea struck a chord within Stan. Could the elders be preparing for a festival?

Konstantine didn't remember any festivals being at this time of year—though Wolfnacht had a very long history, and sometimes an ancient remembrance would catch him unaware.

If they're preparing for a festival, where are the tourists? Stan thought. He tried to find the shapes again, but they'd vanished like specters amid the blowing snow.

Maybe the shapes are tourists on their way to town, Konstantine thought. *Maybe it's some kind of snow festival, and they were waiting for a blizzard.*

The idea seemed unlikely. Few tourists visited Wolfnacht nowadays, and even merchant caravans had become a rare sight. The remaining villagers refused to leave their decaying town, despite the struggles of daily life. Wolfnacht had been a thriving city once, before the Third Wizard War, and none of the remaining elders were willing to admit that those glory days had long past.

Stan knew his people would hang on as long as they could, eking out a marginal living by hunting and farming, rather than retreating to the safety of the Atrian Plains. Stan didn't share their devotion. As soon as he reached his majority, he would leave Wolfnacht and never look back.

"Those shapes aren't tourists," he muttered, not caring that there was no one around to hear him. Not even the bravest merchant or the rowdiest tourist would venture through the mountains during a snowstorm like this.

A chill, entirely unrelated to the weather, ran down Konstantine's spine. Would a blizzard bother *the Enemy*?

Stan didn't know. The elders of Wolfnacht seldom mentioned the supernatural threat lurking beyond the Timberline Mountains, and when they did speak of it, it was always in hushed and furtive tones.

Could this be the Enemy, looking to catch Wolfnacht unaware?

The shapes emerged from the snow again, but this time they weren't at the foot of the mountains—they were much, much closer.

How can anyone move so quickly through this kind of weather? Stan wondered.

The shadows resolved themselves into mounted figures, moving in single file, plowing rapidly through the fresh-fallen snow.

Konstantine hurried toward the alarm bell, near the main gate. He wrapped his hand around the cold, wet pull-cord, but then hesitated.

Maybe it's not the Enemy, he thought. *Better to get a good look at the intruders before stirring up the whole town.* The adolescent took a deep breath to steady his nerves.

Gradually, seven figures emerged from the storm. Clouds of breath and steam rose from the riders, only to be whipped away by the snowy wind. The riders appeared human. They were dressed

61

in heavy cloaks, wearing armor, and carrying weapons. Dirt and blood stained the travelers' clothes; they looked as though they'd been through a war.

Konstantine gaped and his arm dropped away from the alarm bell. It wasn't the warriors that riveted the young man's attention, though; it was their mounts. Though one of the steeds was a simple pack horse, the remaining six animals were *unicorns.*

Stan had never seen anything like the unicorns before. Three were brilliant white, nearly invisible in the storm, save for the blood staining their coats. The fourth was dappled gray, and the fifth shone like gold. Ahead of the rest came a magnificent silver mare with a long, spiral horn protruding from her forehead. The unicorn stopped a respectful distance from the gate, and the lead rider—a big man with a serious face and a drooping moustache—called up to Konstantine.

"You there!" the man said, glowering. "I am Lance Sergeant Carl Volstag of the Sixth Atrian Cavalry, and this is my mount, Stardust. Your village is in dire peril, and my company needs rest and healing. Open your gates and let us in!" The sergeant wore tarnished and dented plate armor and carried a spiked mace.

"Please," added the rider of the gold unicorn, waiting just behind the leader. She shivered slightly as she spoke; she appeared barely older than Konstantine.

Stan couldn't seem to find the words to reply. He gazed at the strange visitors, one after another. Despite their wounds and their weary faces, he had a hard time believing the riders were real. He'd heard tales of the Atrian Cavalry, of course—everyone had—but he'd never seen so much as a single cavalry trooper before in his life. He noticed for the first time that there was a body, bloody and unmoving, slung over the back of the pack horse in the middle of the group.

"Stop gaping and let us in, boy!" Volstag commanded.

"I-I'll have to ask the elders," Stan called back. The riders didn't *seem* evil, and he'd never heard of the Enemy using unicorns before—Could unicorns even become undead? But the arrival of a patrol of Atrian Cavalry in the middle of a blizzard was unlikely as well. Perhaps it was some kind of Enemy trick.

Stan couldn't leave the palisade unmanned with intruders at the gate, so he grabbed hold of the wet, chilly bell cord and pulled. He beat the alarm in a clear, steady rhythm—hoping to convey a sense of urgency, rather than panic, to the people of Wolfnacht.

As the peals echoed above the storm, the doors of Wolfnacht flew open, and the villagers spilled out into the snowy streets. Some people pulled on clothes as they ran, others hefted weapons or buckled up ancient armor. Many of the townsfolk appeared frightened, others seemed curious, and some looked annoyed at being called out on a snowy evening. Many of the townsfolk carried torches and lanterns as they bustled toward the gate.

Berman, the chief elder, spotted Konstantine standing atop the wall and glowered at him. Many of the other villagers glared, too.

"What is it?" Berman called. He finished buttoning his trousers over his large belly and slogged up the palisade stair.

Nikolas, a rangy man with scruffy black hair and a stubbly face, laughed. "It's just my little brother, Konstantine," he barked as he followed Berman up. "Stan's a bit daft. Just havin' some fun with us, I'm sure."

"Well, Konstantine will find I don't have much of a sense of humor on a night like this," Berman said.

"I swear, Elder Berman, this is no jest," Stan said. The wolfish look on his brother's face made Stan's stomach twist.

Sweat dripped down the adolescent's brow and mingled with the melting snow. "I-it's important," he stammered. "We have visitors. Look!" He pointed toward the cavalry below.

Berman frowned and peered over the pointed tops of the logs. When he saw the patrol, his eyes narrowed.

"Hail and well met, Elder Berman," a dark-haired woman on a white unicorn called before the gruff sergeant could speak. "I am

Corporal Lanna of the Sixth Atrian Cavalry, rider of Helios. And this is my commander, Lance Sergeant Carl Volstag, rider of Stardust. He would like to speak to you about a matter of great import." Her tones were compelling, almost musical.

She flashed Volstag a slight smile, and the sergeant's stern expression softened. He straightened regally in his saddle, brushed the snow from the shoulders of his cloak, and said, "Indeed, sir. It is urgent that we speak."

"What do you want?" Berman called down curtly. He didn't look very happy to see either the riders or their unicorns.

"My patrol is in difficult straits," Volstag replied. "We need shelter from this storm and a medic."

"I thought all unicorn riders had their own healers," Nikolas put in suspiciously.

Volstag glowered at Konstantine's brother for a moment before glancing toward an unsteady white stallion. A bloodied young woman wobbled atop the unicorn's back, looking as though she might fall off at any moment.

"Our healer is gravely injured," Sergeant Volstag explained, "as is his rider. Others of our company are wounded, too."

Konstantine's eyes fell on the body slung over the back of the pack horse. Was the man dead? If not, he soon would be.

Elder Berman remained unmoved. He folded his flabby arms across his chest.

"Please," the rider of the golden unicorn interjected. "We need your help!"

"We also bring news about The Enemy," Corporal Lanna added, "intelligence vital to the survival of your people."

Konstantine noticed that she, too, was bloodied and unsteady in the saddle. The dappled unicorn was also hurt. Occasionally, the third white unicorn rider or the golden rider would move close and steady one of their injured comrades.

By now, more villagers had made their way to the top of the palisade. Many of them jostled past Stan, pushing the youngster back so that he could barely see over the parapet.

"Turn them away," urged Mapes, a newly arrived elder. Her steely blue eyes glistened in the lantern light. "We can spare neither the time nor the supplies to take care of lost sheep—or unicorns."

"She's right," Nikolas agreed. "We've got too much to do. They'll only get in the way."

"But we are Atrian Cavalry!" the young woman on the golden unicorn blurted. "We protect this village and *every* part of Atrios!"

"The only thing we need protection from is vagabonds like you," Mapes shot back.

"I agree," added Zurko, the butcher. "The cavalry's done nothing for us. Now, suddenly, in the dead of winter—the day before the anniversary—they appear on our doorstep asking favors? Outrageous!"

"Aye," Nikolas sneered. "They may ride unicorns, but they're still just beggars. We should turn them away."

Volstag reddened, about to give an angry reply, but Lanna cut him off.

"We will gladly pay for the services you render," she offered.

"Pay with what?" Zurko asked. "Promises you won't keep? We know about cavalry promises. The mountains are littered with dead villages promised much by the cavalry."

"We'll not be taken in by such tricks," Mapes added.

"We'll pay with gold!" Volstag bellowed.

"Or silver, if you prefer," Lanna added calmly.

II. Welcome to Wolfnacht

All at once, the villagers began babbling excitedly. The five elders—Berman, Mapes, Zurko, Bev the herbalist, and Thynes the scribe—huddled together, whispering to each other. Nikolas stood at the edge of the group, listening attentively, his dark eyes darting from the elders to the unicorn riders and back.

Stan strained his ears, trying to overhear, but he only caught a few snatches of conversation.

"*Real* money could be useful . . ."

". . . so close to the ceremony . . ."

". . . the anniversary is for *us*, not outsiders . . ."

". . . a sign from the gods . . ."

". . . no reason to turn them away . . ."

". . . might be exactly what we need."

As the elders conferred, Volstag leaned over and said something to Lanna. Her face remained impassive, but she nodded as he whispered. Konstantine wondered what the riders would do if Berman didn't give in. The golden stallion and his female rider kept moving around the edges of the group, supporting first one of their comrades and then another. Konstantine caught the young rider's eye; she looked as nervous as he felt.

The elders broke their huddle. "Open the gates!" Berman announced.

As the huge wooden doors swung open, the battered cavalry members let out a collective sigh of relief. Stan, who didn't even realize he'd been holding his breath, exhaled also.

Berman and the others made their way down from the wall and greeted the riders as the cavalry entered Wolfnacht. Stan followed and pushed to the front of the crowd as the villagers made way for the unicorns.

"You mentioned gold," Berman said, stepping boldly in front of Volstag's mount, forcing the unicorn to halt.

The sergeant pulled a small pouch from his belt and tossed it into Berman's hand. Mapes took the bag from Berman, opened it, and dipped her head in approval. Berman bowed and stepped out of the way, though Stan thought the elder's smile disingenuous.

The townspeople walked ahead of the riders, leading the cavalry through Wolfnacht's winding streets.

"We can put you up in the inn," Berman said, "though I'm afraid it's rather dusty. We don't get too many visitors this time of year."

The rider on the dappled unicorn—a man with curly black hair and a moustache—shook his head. "It's a wonder you have any visitors at all, if this is how you treat them." His unicorn neighed in agreement, but stumbled slightly in the snow. A white unicorn with an injured rider on her back stepped forward and propped up the dappled rider.

"We're sorry to appear so suspicious," Thynes, the scribe, said rubbing his bony hands together. "But tomorrow is an important anniversary for us, and outsiders are not allowed at the *Festival of Wolfnacht*—not usually, anyway."

As the group continued toward the inn, Konstantine pressed closer. So there *was* a festival! One he'd never heard of. That explained the elders' furtive preparations.

Volstag seemed unmoved, but the golden unicorn rider asked, "What is the Festival of Wolfnacht?"

"It celebrates the savior of our village, Olen Wolfnacht," Elder Bev explained. "He was a great hero who slew the mountain bandits threatening our people."

"With the Enemy skulking nearby, the festival is very important to us," Elder Zurko added, "and we can only celebrate on the anniversary of Wolfnacht's victory."

"The Enemy is closer than you know," Volstag said grimly. "An army of zombies and fell creatures ambushed us on the other side of the Wolfnacht Pass."

"We barely escaped with our lives," added the curly-haired rider of the dappled unicorn.

The townspeople stopped suddenly, hemming the riders in. For a moment, the only sound was the howling of the wind.

"So you've led the Enemy *here*?" Mapes shrieked.

"The dark forces were coming anyway," Lanna told her. "Tomorrow is the *Vanishing Eclipse*—one of the times the Enemy is strongest. We believe that they will storm the pass and sweep through the mountains into this land, if not during tomorrow's eclipse, then very soon."

Volstag puffed out his chest. "You should evacuate the village as soon as possible. My patrol will leave to fetch reinforcements as soon as we are able."

"The storm gods willing," added the dappled unicorn rider.

The crowd bust into worried murmurs. "But what about our homes?" "What about our farms?" "We can't just leave!" "Tomorrow is the Festival!" "This is our town!" "This is our life!"

Stan's stomach lurched. Had *he* sensed the supernatural forces gathering on the other side of the Wolfnacht pass? Was this the unnamable dread that had called him out into the storm?

Berman raised his hands to quiet the crowd. "Now, now," he said. "There's no need to worry. We elders have anticipated this . . . *Vanishing*, as the riders call it, for some time. Why, Olen Wolfnacht's greatest deeds were accomplished on just such a day. It was during the dark moments of *Nyarra's Rebirth*, long ago, that Wolfnacht himself destroyed our village's enemies."

"That is why we planned the Festival for this sacred time," Mapes added. "It is the only time the rites will do any good. When the sun goes dark, our village has nothing to fear from anyone. Our celebration of the *Festival of Wolfnacht* will keep us safe for generations to come."

The unicorn riders exchanged skeptical looks.

"Perhaps we can discuss this on the morrow," Corporal Lanna suggested.

"Yes," Zurko, the butcher, replied. "Plenty of time on the morrow."

"The key is for every Wolfnachter to keep working," Thynes added. "All the arrangements must be complete." The scribe's aged face gazed out over the townsfolk. Many grinned their approval, but some of the younger villagers seemed just as confused as Stan.

"Speaking of arrangements," Lanna said diplomatically, "our patrol needs to rest and recuperate. I'm not saying your festival won't work its magic, but if it *doesn't* you'll need the cavalry to protect you."

Berman and the elders merely smiled. The crowd parted once more, and the riders crossed the last few hundred yards to the inn, an old timber-frame building with plaster walls and a thatched roof. A tumble-down stable stood next door; both structures were deserted.

The unicorns and their riders eyed the accommodations warily.

Berman beamed. "The best the town has to offer," he said.

"Thanks," said the curly haired rider, though Stan didn't think he meant it.

As the patrol dismounted, most of the villagers—save for the elders—hurried back to their homes. The blizzard was still blowing, and few cared to brave the storm any longer just to gawk at the ragged cavalry.

Konstantine remained, patting his arms to ward off the chill.

"I'm afraid you'll have to look after yourselves," Mapes told the riders. "The innkeeper and his wife are busy with preparations for the festival—like everyone else."

"What about the stable hands?" Volstag asked.

"He died of flu earlier this year," Elder Bev explained.

"Not enough folk to do the work around here," Berman added jovially. "Sorry."

"I can help," Konstantine blurted. "I'd love to help."

Nikolas glared at his younger brother. "What about your chores, boy?"

"I can do them later," Stan shot back. Nikolas stepped forward and raised his arm to strike his brother, but Berman stepped between them.

The Elder scratched his chin. "I suppose we could spare *one* of our young people to help you riders out."

"Thank you," Lanna said. She winced and gripped her left shoulder. Konstantine noticed fresh blood seeping through her cloak.

The eyes of all five elders fastened on the corporal. Some looked concerned, but others—perhaps still worried about the threat to the village—appeared to be taking the measure of the wounded riders.

"Yes. Thanks," Volstag added, keeping his eyes fixed on Berman. "We appreciate it."

Berman bowed politely as he and the other elders turned to leave. "I'll see if I can turn up another youngster to help you," he said. "But don't count on it. All of us are very busy, you know."

"So we've heard," the curly haired rider of the dappled unicorn muttered.

"Keep out of trouble, colt," Nikolas said, cuffing Konstantine on the back of the head.

Stan glared at his brother. "Worry about yourself, why don't you?"

Nikolas and the elders chuckled and walked away.

"I will bring herbs," Bev, the herbalist, called back over her shoulder. "I'm no Il-Siha, but perhaps some of my remedies may bring you relief."

"Thank you," the golden unicorn's rider called after her.

"Thanks for everything," Lanna added. As the elders left, she and the other riders turned and stared at Konstantine.

For a moment, Stan felt as though he might wither under their collective gaze.

"Can we trust you, boy?" Volstag asked gruffly.

"I . . . Of course!" Stan replied.

"I don't see we have any choice," Lanna's white unicorn, Helios, muttered.

Konstantine's legs buckled and he plopped down into the snow. "It . . . it talks!"

"So do *you*," Helios replied, "but you don't see me making an ass of myself about it."

"Do all unicorns talk?" Stan asked, wide-eyed.

"Yes," the golden unicorn nearby told him. "But some only talk to their riders."

His rider, the young blond woman, helped Konstantine to his feet. "I'm Private First Class Kyra," she said. "And this is Rigel." She patted her mount on his golden neck.

"K-Konstantine," the boy managed to stammer. "Most people call me Stan." He extended his hand again, and Kyra shook it.

"Enough chatter," Volstag said. "People are bleeding to death here, boy. Make yourself useful or get out of the way."

To Stan, the entire patrol appeared much more beat up than they had just moments before: their shoulders sagged, their eyes looked tired and worried, and they clutched at their still-bleeding wounds and gritted their teeth against the pain of their injuries. Clearly, the riders had been hiding the extent of their wounds from Berman and the Wolfnacht elders.

A ginger-haired youth in the back of the group lolled forward, leaning heavily against his white unicorn's neck. At the front, a woman with mousy brown hair swayed precariously, and her eyes rolled back in her head.

Stan and Kyra rushed forward and caught her before she fell. As they draped her arms around their shoulders and helped her down, the unicorn she'd been riding collapsed into the snow. Dark blood seeped from beneath the unicorn's white mane.

"Percy's down!" Kyra announced. "And Janise isn't in much better shape." She and Stan struggled to keep the wounded rider, Janise, on her feet.

"Get her inside," Volstag ordered. He and Lanna had gone to help the unconscious rider slung over the pack horse. "Rigel can help Santos and Apollonia with Percy. Lanna and I will do what we can for Wilfred."

Rigel, Kyra's golden mount, bobbed his head in agreement.

"Luva's tears!" Volstag cursed. "Stardust warned me that this place would be trouble!"

The ginger-haired young man righted himself. "Where *hasn't* been trouble for us lately, Sarge?" he said. Then he broke into a coughing fit.

"Are you okay, Roj?" Kyra asked, concern written across her young face.

Roj nodded, but couldn't manage to say anything through the coughing. His unicorn didn't look in much better shape; her knees buckled slightly as she tried to support her rider.

"Volstag and I will help Roj and Cherish once we've looked after Wilfred," Lanna assured Kyra. "You concentrate on Janise."

"I'm fine," Roj gasped, but none of the rest believed him.

Lanna and Volstag carefully lifted the badly wounded man, Wilfred, from the back of the pack horse. As they did, bells attached to the animal's harness jingled softly.

Stan paused as he and Kyra helped Janise toward the inn. *So that's the sound I heard through the storm,* he thought. The cheerful noise sounded completely inappropriate given the current situation.

Sergeant Volstag scowled. "And keep that boy out of the way," he ordered Kyra.

"Yes, sir," she replied. "Come on, Stan. Let's get Janise inside."

Konstantine helped walk the wounded rider inside the inn. Kyra's blue eyes scanned the great room and settled on a padded chair by the fireplace. "We'll sit her down there," she told Stan.

At that moment, Janise's legs gave way. Stan staggered under the sudden burden, but Kyra supported most of the weight, and they soon managed to drag Janise to the chair. As they set her down, the brown-haired rider's head lolled from side to side. Her deep brown eyes stared blankly at the ceiling, and her mouth gaped. Kyra lifted Janise's cloak, revealing a blood-soaked tunic beneath.

Kyra pulled a silver knife from her boot and cut open the fabric covering Janise's right side. A ragged gash, just above the hip, oozed dark blood.

Stan gasped and went pale.

"Don't pass out on me, Konstantine," Kyra muttered, still cutting.

He shook his head, fighting back swirling nausea. "I won't."

"Good. Get me some hot water and fresh cloth to clean the wound."

Stan peered around, but the fire in the inn's hearth was merely a few smoldering coals. "There's no fire," he said plaintively. "And I don't see any clean cloth, either."

"There must be bedspreads somewhere in this gods-forsaken place," Kyra said. "Tear some up—but make sure they've been washed recently."

"Okay," Stan said. He turned toward the stairs leading to the guest rooms.

"Oh," Kyra called after him. "Throw me something strong from the bar. Cleaning the wound with alcohol will have to suffice until you can get the fire going."

"Right," he said. He took a bottle of whiskey from behind the counter and tossed it to her, then hurried to the stairs.

As he ascended, she uncorked the bottle with her teeth. "Sorry about this, Janise," Kyra said, pouring the alcohol on her comrade's wound. Janise screamed.

The horrible cry echoed in Stan's ears as he raced upstairs. Heart pounding, he ransacked three guest rooms before finding a

73

set of clean sheets. He yanked the linens from the bed and tore them into strips as he rushed back downstairs.

Janise lay slumped unconscious in the chair, with Kyra still examining her side. The other riders had brought the badly wounded man, Wilfred, into the room and laid him on a table near the fireplace. Sergeant Volstag, Corporal Lanna, ginger-haired Roj, and the rider with curly black hair crouched around their fallen comrade, tending the hideous wounds that covered Wilfred's body.

"Thanks," Kyra said as Stan handed her the strips of clean cloth. "Now see what you can do about that fire."

Stan fetched some logs from beside the hearth and shoved them into the fireplace. The rough bark scraped against his skin, but he was glad for it. The sensation distracted him from the nauseating stench of blood and guts that now filled the room.

With skill born from long practice, Konstantine quickly built the smoldering embers into a strong blaze. He stood, triumphant, and smiled—but the expression faded when he saw the riders' grim faces. All of them, even Kyra, now stood around Wilfred; they hung their heads.

"Dammit!" Roj said. "There must be something more we can do!" His breath came in ragged gasps.

Lanna shook her head and Kyra brushed back a tear. "No," Volstag announced. "There's nothing."

"I'm sorry, Roj," Lanna said. "He's gone."

Stan swallowed hard. The dead man lay pale and motionless on the table. The terrible wounds across his chest and belly glistened red in the firelight. Stan's stomach twisted. He'd seen dead bodies before, but never anyone killed by violence.

"It's better this way," the curly haired rider said. "He wouldn't have wanted to live with Fiona gone—same as I wouldn't want to carry on without Apollonia."

Roj staggered toward him, but Kyra stepped between them.

"Easy for you to say, Santos," Roj snapped. "Apollonia's not lying dead in that gods-cursed pass, swarmed by zombies like Fiona."

Santos' dark eyes flared. "You think I don't know that?" he snapped back. "All of us were lucky to get out of that pass alive. I thank the gods that Apollonia was only wounded. But if she'd fallen, I'd have wanted you to leave me there at her side. We should have done the same for Wilfred."

"You're saying we should have left him there, even though he was still alive?" Roj said. He began coughing again.

"Better to die in battle than in some flea-bitten inn," Santos replied.

"Enough!" Volstag barked. "There'll be no more talk of dying while I'm in charge. We're going to tend our wounded and return to base, every last one of us. Kyra, how's Janise?"

Kyra took a deep breath. The flickering firelight behind her turned Kyra's pale blond hair into a glowing halo. To Stan, the young rider looked like a warrior angel.

"She's in bad shape," Kyra said. "There was a zombie finger joint still lodged in her side, but I removed it. I've cleansed the area with alcohol and holy water—but I'm no Il-Siha medic. If infection doesn't set in, she might pull through." The girl appeared sad and very tired. "What about Percy?"

Lanna pulled her soggy cloak back from her face, revealing short dark hair and slightly pointed ears.

She's an elf, Stan thought. *Or a half-elf, anyway.*

The elfish corporal gazed toward the front door, as though listening. "Helios says Percy is in very bad shape," Lanna said. "His powers are failing, and he can't even heal himself. The others aren't sure if he'll last the night."

"What about Apollonia and the rest?" Santos asked. He worriedly smeared the sweat from his brow and pushed his dark, curly hair back on his forehead.

"Helios doesn't think Apollonia's in danger," Lanna said. "If Percy were well, he could heal her up quickly. The others are fine, only minor scrapes and bruises."

"By the Gods of Wrath!" Roj blurted. "Lieutenant Grimshanks and Clementine, Fiona, and now Percy! It's like those undead bastards targeted our healers specifically!"

"They're just zombies," Santos replied. "They can't tell a healer from a hole in the snow."

"Someone's directing them," Kyra said quietly. "Someone's driving that horde through Wolfnacht Pass straight toward this village."

Volstag shook his head. "The Enemy is like a ravenous beast," he said. "It doesn't need a plan; it just devours everything in its path."

A cold shock leapt down Stan's spine. "W-wait!" he gasped. "You mean they're *that* close? The enemy forces that attacked you are *in* Wolfnacht Pass? They didn't attack you while you were trying to reach the pass on the other side? They're not staying on that side of the mountain?"

Santos glared at him. "Weren't you listening, boy? They've massed for invasion, and they're on their way! What do you think we were trying to tell your elders?"

"But it's the middle of a blizzard!" Stan protested.

"The storm didn't stop us coming," Santos said, "and it won't stop the Enemy either."

"They're already dead," Roj muttered. "They don't feel the cold." Pale and sweating, he leaned heavily against one of the room's support posts. Blood dripped down his right arm.

Stan felt as though the whole world might cave in at any moment. "But we need to do something!"

"We *are* doing something," Lanna said calmly. "We're tending our wounded and planning our next move. Kyra, take a look at Roj, would you?"

Kyra stepped toward him, but Roj pulled away, saying, "I'm okay."

Kyra fixed her blue eyes on him. "One infected wound and you're fighting *for* the Enemy instead of against him," she said. Reluctantly, Roj offered his wounded arm for her to examine.

Konstantine wanted to run. He wanted to bolt out into the night and keep running until the snowstorm swallowed him. How could the riders remain so calm with the Enemy nearly at the gates of Wolfnacht?

Volstag put a reassuring hand on Stan's shoulder. "Talk to your people, if you think it'll do any good," the sergeant told the adolescent. "Maybe they'll listen to you better than they listened to us."

All of Stan's breath rushed out at once; he shook his head. "No," he said plaintively. "No one ever listens to me. I'm too young."

"You're old enough to help us," Kyra said, dabbing Roj's wound with a torn sheet. "We have hurt soldiers and injured unicorns to look after. How's that water coming?"

Stan glanced toward the kettle simmering on the fireplace. "Nearly boiling."

"Then fetch it here," she replied. He did, being careful not to burn his fingers on the hot metal.

"Strip down, everyone," Volstag commanded. "I want a full account of wounds. We need to make sure that no one's infected. No one's going over to *their* side, not while I'm in command!"

III. Night at the Inn

Elder Bev returned with her herbs in the middle of the bandaging. She offered a few suggestions for the use of her medicines and then quietly slipped back into the snowy night.

Lanna and Volstag made a quick assessment of the new supplies. They finished re-dressing and, together with Santos, headed for the stable to help the unicorns.

"I'll go with you," Roj offered. Despite his freshly bandaged arm, he still appeared weak and pale.

"No," Lanna said. "Get some rest. Cherish is in better shape than you are; she can help nurse the others."

It seemed as though Roj might not obey, but Volstag turned to Kyra. "Keep him here and make sure he sleeps," he commanded. "Knock him out, if you have to."

"Yessir," Kyra said. Roj glared at her, but the look in the blond girl's eyes told him that—if she had to—she would follow the sergeant's orders to the letter.

"I'll be upstairs," Roj grumbled. "Call if you need me." Kyra nodded, and the ginger-haired young man limped up the stairs to one of the empty bedrooms.

The fire guttered as Volstag, Lanna, and Santos opened the inn door and crossed to the stables. Stan shut the door behind them, closing out the wind, and the fire blazed up again.

Kyra let out a long sigh and slumped into a chair by the fireplace. She gazed at Janise, who slept restlessly nearby.

Stan flopped down on the floor next to Kyra, feeling the warmth of the fire against his skin. Irresistibly, the boy found his gaze drawn toward the ceiling. Before Elder Bev arrived, the cavalry riders had stowed Wilfred's body upstairs.

"Won't he . . ." Stan began. "Won't he become one of *them*?"

Kyra shook her head. "No. Sergeant Volstag will have staked a silver knife through Fred's heart. That, a few prayers, and some holy water should keep Wilfred from troubling us."

"Was he your friend? Wilfred, I mean?"

Kyra ran her hands through her silvery blond hair, closed her eyes, and let her head slump back. "They were all my friends: Lieutenant Grimshanks and Clementine, Fred and Fiona, Vinson and Prys, West, Permichael . . . every one of them, friends as well as comrades. That's the way it is here . . . the way it is for all of us. The Atrian Cavalry isn't just a job, you know—it's a way of life."

"You're not much older than me," Stan said. "You can't have been at it very long."

"Long enough," Kyra replied. "You'd be surprised how long." She slitted her eyes open and looked at Janise. "I pray to the gods that we don't lose anyone else today."

Stan's eyes strayed from the wounded rider to the door. The storm hissed as wind spattered big snowflakes against the swirled panes of glass set into the wooden portal.

"What happened to your patrol?" he asked. "I thought unicorns could heal from any wound. I thought their riders were invincible."

Kyra chuckled ruefully. "It's nice that some people still believe those myths," she said. "We're better trained and equipped than most warriors, but in the end, we're just as mortal as anyone else—as you've seen."

"Yes." Stan said. It was more a sigh than a word, and his head sagged with disappointment. "So, what happened? Did the Enemy take you by surprise?"

Her blue eyes stared off into an uncertain distance. "They caught us in the pass as we were returning from patrol. There were hundreds of them, thousands maybe, concealed in the rocks. They pulled Lieutenant Grimshanks and Clementine down almost before we realized what was happening.

"The rest of us fought like hell, but it was all we could do to break away and save ourselves. The others—the ones we lost—bought our escape with their lives." She glanced toward the door, and, at that moment, a high, keening wail pierced the snowy darkness.

"What's that?" Stan asked, jumping to his feet.

Kyra quickly knelt at Janise's side. The unconscious girl writhed in her chair. It was all the blond rider could do to hold her wounded friend down.

"Percy's gone," Kyra explained. She bowed her head and tears dripped down her face.

"How do you know?" Stan asked. "Do you have some kind of telepathic bond with your unicorn, like that elf girl does?" He was guessing about Lanna's power, but, given what he'd seen, it was a reasonable surmise.

"I don't need telepathy for this," Kyra snapped. "Can't you hear it? That's the unicorn's death song. They only sing it when they've lost one of their own."

"I'm sorry," Konstantine said. He felt a fool—completely inadequate next to this strong, brave, beautiful girl.

Kyra's expression softened. "Just help me to hold Janise down until the fits pass," she said.

Konstantine knelt beside her and helped keep the wounded rider in the chair. Janise was surprisingly strong, given her condition. "Will she be all right?" Stan asked.

"Losing a unicorn is like losing part of your own body," Kyra replied. "Some people *never* recover from it. If we can get her through the night, she might stand a chance." In Kyra's startling blue eyes, Stan saw determination and just a hint of fear. But was it fear for herself, or for her friend?

"How long do you think we have?" he asked quietly.

"How long until Janise is okay?"

"No—how long until the enemy comes."

"No way of knowing. Not tonight, I hope, but anytime in the next few days. We dealt them a blow, though it cost us dearly, but we haven't delayed them for long. I hope this magic ritual your elders are planning to protect the town works."

"I . . . I hope so, too."

"How are they going to do it? Do you know?"

Konstantine squirmed and turned away from her piercing gaze. "I really don't know anything," he said. "I'm not old enough, you see. That's what *they* think, anyway."

Janise's struggling had lessened, and Kyra put a steady hand on Stan's shoulder.

"I was younger than you when I joined the cavalry," the girl with the silver-blond hair said. "There's more in you than your elders give you credit for."

"It might not be so bad if my parents were alive," Stan said. "But Nikolas ... my brother ... he likes to treat me like a child. It makes him feel older, I suppose."

She bobbed her head sympathetically. "I lost my parents, too. What can you tell me about this hero your town is named after?"

"They say that on the day of *Nyarra's Rebirth*, Olen Wolfnacht made a pact with the gods. The gods gave him the power to protect the village from its enemies," Stan replied. "They say Wolfnacht drove the bandits back into the mountains and killed their chief. Then he tamed all the surrounding countryside and made Wolfnacht safe. At least . . . until the war."

"Is that what the elders are going to do tomorrow? Are they going to renew the town's pact with the gods?"

"Maybe. I don't know. The temple in town is deserted."

Kyra frowned.

"The priest died a few years ago, and they never sent a replacement," Stan explained, feeling the paucity of the excuse as he said it. "I heard my brother say, 'The gods abandoned Wolfnacht long ago.'" He took a deep breath. "I heard other people say the same thing about the Atrian Cavalry."

"We didn't abandon you," Kyra said. "If we had, we wouldn't have been riding patrol in the mountains."

"Maybe it would have been better for you if you *had* abandoned us." He hung his head.

81

Kyra put her hand under his chin and lifted his face to hers. "We will *never* desert those in need," she said. "I promise you."

Konstantine turned away. He believed her, but he also knew that sometimes people couldn't help breaking well-intended promises. Sometimes circumstances intervened, and people didn't have any more choice than his parents—or the town priest—had.

Janise had ceased struggling, so Kyra had Stan fetch down some clean bedding and pillows from the guest rooms. The two of them fixed up a makeshift bed near the fireplace and gently lowered the wounded girl onto it. Kyra tucked up the covers tight around Janise, wiped the sweat from her friend's face, and kissed the unconscious girl on the forehead.

"You sleep now," the silver-haired warrior said gently.

Just at that moment, the door blew open and the other riders entered. They slammed the door shut, stomped the snow from their boots, and stripped off their sodden cloaks.

"You heard?" Volstag asked.

"Aye," Kyra said.

"We have a difficult decision to make," the sergeant said.

"What decision?" she asked.

"Roj and Lanna are pretty badly hurt—" Volstag began. When Lanna started to protest, he cut her off. "—Even if our half-elf friend here won't admit it. She and Roj need rest—a lot of it. Apollonia shouldn't be traveling, either. You, Santos, and I are pretty banged up also, as are our mounts."

"We're well enough to ride," Kyra said. "We could go for help."

"Yes, the three of us are well enough to ride," Volstag admitted, "but we're not going to leave without our comrades. And we can't stay in this doomed village any more than the townsfolk can, not with the Enemy surging through that pass at any moment."

"Maybe the magic spell the villagers are planning will work," Santos suggested. "Maybe it will keep the undead at bay."

"Are you willing to bet your life on that, Santos?" Volstag said. "Because I'm not."

"So, what can you do?" Stan asked. Everyone but Kyra jumped; they'd forgotten the boy was in the room.

"Yes," Kyra said, "what can we do?"

"We can try to make a potion from Percy's horn," Lanna said wearily. "He had the gift of healing. Even in death, he could pass it along to us."

"But Permichael and West are dead," Kyra said. "None of us have the skill to brew such a potion."

"I can try," Lanna replied. "I've seen it done before—once."

"It's not much of a chance," Volstag admitted.

The half-elf corporal sighed. "It's the only chance we've got."

"Unless the villagers' ceremony works," Santos put in. All of the riders stared at Stan, as though expecting him to know about the planned ceremony.

The adolescent squirmed under their gaze. "I don't know," he said. "I-I hope it will work."

"The elders haven't let him in on their plans," Kyra explained.

"We have to try using the horn," Lanna insisted. "I don't like desecrating Percy's body any more than the rest of you do, but. . . ."

Slowly, Kyra bowed her head. "We'll need all our strength if we have to fight to protect the villagers."

"You'd do that?" Stan said. "Even after the way they treated you?"

"It's our duty, boy!" Santos replied.

Volstag crossed his arms over his barrel-like chest. "We'll have to keep our mounts calm while extracting the horn," he explained. "They understand the necessity of it, but it still won't be easy for them."

"No easier than cutting up Wilfred would be for us," Lanna added. Stan shuddered at the thought.

"What about Roj and Janise?" Kyra asked.

"Gods willing, they'll sleep through the whole thing," Volstag replied.

"How can I help?" Stan asked.

Volstag glowered at him. "Just keep out of the way," the leader of the unicorn riders said.

"And tell us if there's any change in Janise or Roj," Kyra said, flashing Stan a sympathetic smile. "Please." She donned her cloak and the others did the same.

"How long will . . . extracting the horn take?" Stan asked as the riders opened the door. Outside, the wind howled hungrily.

"Hours, probably," Lanna replied. "If the magic is to work at all, the extraction has to be done correctly."

"Don't wait up," Santos added grimly.

The riders went out to the stables, pulling the door shut behind them. Outside, the blizzard howled and scratched at the windowpanes.

IV. Into the Cold

Konstantine bundled a soft quilt around his shoulders, settled back in a big wooden chair, and stared into the fire. He wished he could assist the riders in some way—they were trying to save his people, after all—but what else could he do? He didn't know what kind of spell the elders were planning for Nyarra's Rebirth, and he certainly didn't know anything about unicorn horns or potions.

He glanced at Janise, slumbering next to the hearth. She looked terrible. Even in sleep, worry furrowed her pale, sweaty brow. Every now and again, she twitched and groaned softly. Stan wished he were a healer, or, at the least, that he'd taken lessons in palliative herbs from Elder Bev.

Outside, the wind continued to wail, and snowflakes scraped and spattered against the inn's windowpanes. But inside, by the fire, the room was warm and the air close and comforting. As Stan waited for the other riders to return, exhaustion took him and his eyes slowly drifted shut.

He dreamed he was sitting in the common room of the inn, just as he had been when he fell asleep. Outside, the blizzard still raged, but there was a new noise, too. The howling that filled the inn wasn't just the wind anymore, it was hungry wolves, prowling outside—the Enemy's corpse wolves, looking for a chink in Wolfnacht's defenses.

But hadn't wolves been the totem animals of Olen Wolfnacht, too? Stan thought so, though his sleep-beclouded mind couldn't be sure. He thought he remembered stories of the town's founder wearing wolfskins and leading twin gray wolves into battle.

Perhaps that's what Stan was hearing; perhaps it wasn't the Enemy outside, but Wolfnacht himself coming to rescue the people of his village.

As Stan stared at the window, hoping beyond hope that the ancient hero was arriving, something stirred by the hearth. Stan swiveled in his chair just as Janise rose from her bundled blankets.

She was tall and fair, naked—her skin pale and her brown hair golden in the firelight. She didn't seem wounded at all; she looked like a shimmering goddess.

Stan made to stand up and help her, but she shook her head and put a finger to her lips. Wordlessly, she walked across the common room, opened, the door, and vanished into the snowy night. Outside, the wolves howled more loudly—apparently overjoyed to see her.

Konstantine smiled, glad that Janise had recovered. He pulled his quilts around him and settled back to sleep. But, oddly, he felt cold.

Why was it so cold here by the fire?

"Konstantine! Konstantine, wake up!"

Kyra stood over him, worry etched across her young face. She stepped nimbly out of the way as Volstag's strong hands reached past her and seized Konstantine by the shirtfront.

Volstag lifted Stan out of the chair and shook him. "Where's Janise?" the sergeant demanded, his face purple with rage. "Where is she, you foolish boy?"

"I . . . I don't know!" Stan gasped. He glanced toward the fire; the wounded girl was gone, just as in his dream. Volstag dropped him back into the chair.

Near the door, Lanna bent low to the floorboards, examining some dark, wet stains on the wood—blood or melted snow. "She must have gone," the half-elf said. "She must have walked into the storm while we were . . . working."

"She's delirious," Santos put in. "The loss of Percy must have unhinged her. Better riders than Janise have lost their minds when their steeds died."

"Damn it to the abyss!" Volstag cursed.

"We have to find her," Kyra said urgently. "She won't last long in this storm."

"I-I'll help," Stan said. The thought of the injured rider wandering alone in the blizzard twisted his stomach into worried knots.

Volstag, Lanna, and Santos glared at him. "You've already done enough," Santos snarled.

"It's not his fault," Kyra said, stepping between her friends and the young man. "You told him to get some sleep, Santos. How could he know Janise would wander off? Besides, Konstantine knows this area better than we do. Maybe he *can* help."

"Yes," Konstantine said. "Yes, I want to help. Please!"

"He's your responsibility, then," Volstag said, thrusting his index finger toward the silver-haired girl. "You, Lanna, and I will mount up. Santos, you administer the potion to Roj and Apollonia. Then you and she will follow us. Cherish can stand guard outside the inn and make sure Roj doesn't wander off before he's fully healed."

The other members of the patrol saluted and said, "Yessir!"

Kyra took Stan by the elbow. "Grab your cloak," she said. "You'll be riding behind me on Rigel. He's strong, and the extra weight won't bother him."

Stan fetched his cloak and boots from where they'd been drying by the fire. In less than two minutes, he and Kyra were out the door and into the blizzard.

Riding a unicorn was a lot like riding a horse—though Konstantine didn't have much experience with that, either. The unicorns didn't have saddles, so Stan perched himself on Rigel's back, just behind Kyra, and locked his arms around her waist. Pressing against the quiver of crossbow bolts strapped to the girl warrior's back was uncomfortable, but she felt very warm, and the strength of her body reassured him. Riding with Kyra of the silvery hair, he would be safe.

Kyra, Rigel, and Stan formed up outside the stable with Volstag and Stardust, and Lanna and Helios. Cherish went to stand guard in front of the inn, while Santos—having administered the potion to his steed, Apollonia—headed inside to heal Roj.

Lanna checked the snow for tracks and led the other riders toward Wolfnacht's main gate.

"Are you sure she went the way?" Volstag asked, peering into the snowstorm.

"With the wind blurring the tracks, I can't tell for certain," Lanna replied. "Where else could she be, though? If she were wandering in the village, someone would have found her and brought her back to us by now."

"The villagers haven't been very helpful so far," Kyra noted.

It's that damn festival! Stan thought, feeling deeply ashamed. *Everyone in Wolfnacht is too busy preparing for the Nyarra's Rebirth. A wounded girl is wandering alone in the snow, and none of my people have even noticed!*

As the riders approached the gate, a lithe shadow appeared out of the snowy darkness and blocked their way.

"Nikolas!" Konstantine said, recognizing his brother.

"Where do all of you think you're going?" Nikolas asked. "Sneaking off like thieves in the night?" He scowled at the three unicorns and their riders from beneath his thick, dark brows.

"One of our riders has gone missing," Volstag said gruffly.

"She was injured," Lanna explained. "Delirious. She's wandered off into the storm."

"Did you see anyone leave, Nikolas?" Kyra asked.

Nikolas' eyes narrowed. "We heard a commotion and the elders sent me out to check," he said. "I found *you* prowling around. I haven't seen any girl."

"What about the guards?" Kyra said. "Didn't you leave someone guarding the wall after we arrived? Did they see anyone?"

"Wolfnacht is a large town," he replied. "And, with the festival tomorrow, we could only spare one person for the walls. Probably he's walking some other section of the palisade."

"So someone could have sneaked out," Lanna pressed.

"It's possible," Nikolas said, shrugging. "But no one will be leaving while I'm here." He smirked and bowed impudently.

To Stan, the smile seemed like a threat. How his brother might stop the powerful unicorn riders, Stan couldn't imagine. Nikolas was slowing them down when every moment counted.

Stan slid from Rigel's back and stood face to face with his brother. "They're trying to help," Stan said. "Don't you understand that?"

Nikolas grinned at him. "Are you the unicorn riders' *pet* now, Stan?"

"No more than you're the pet of Berman and Mapes," Stan shot back.

Nikolas' right fist smashed into Konstantine's chin.

The world exploded into a cascade of falling stars, and Stan toppled back into the snow. He landed hard on his rump. Nikolas seized Stan by the shirt and reeled back for another blow.

Before the punch fell, Kyra snagged Nikolas' wrist. Her blue eyes stared coldly at him. He sneered at her.

"If you know what's good for you, you'll leave him alone and let us pass," she said.

"So . . . *that's* how it is," Nikolas snarled.

"That's how it is," she replied.

Nikolas shook himself free and backed away. Stan staggered to his feet, wiping a trickle of blood from his mouth.

"You can leave, if you want," Nikolas told the group, as he pulled back one side of the gate, "but don't expect to be let back in." He fixed his eyes upon his younger brother. "*None* of you."

"We'll see about that when the time comes," Volstag said. He urged Stardust through the gap and into the snowy wilderness beyond. Lanna on Helios followed, with Kyra and Stan on Rigel bringing up the rear.

Stan's gaze lingered on the gates of Wolfnacht as he rode away.

"Worried about leaving—or about returning?" Kyra asked.

"Neither," he replied. "I was just hoping my brother wouldn't bother the other riders when they try to follow us."

"Don't worry," Kyra said. "Santos and Apollonia can take care of themselves."

They'd ridden several hundred yards toward the mountains now, but the darkness and the swirling snow was making it nearly impossible to see.

"Janise!" Volstag called, but the wail of the storm smothered even the sergeant's booming voice. "Can you and Helios see anything, Lanna?"

"Not a trace," she replied. "The snow blows away the tracks as soon as we make them. If Percy were still alive, Helios might be able to track Janise telepathically, but. . . ." She shrugged her hands helplessly.

"Fingall's balls!" Volstag cursed. "We'll have to split up."

"I-is that safe?" Stan asked.

"There's no other choice," Volstag said. "We either find Janise quickly, or she freezes to death."

"Dawn's only a few hours away," Kyra pointed out.

"It won't come soon enough to save her," Lanna replied. "Janise is tough, but, without Percy, she won't last long out here."

"Stardust and I will bull our way north, toward the pass," Volstag said. "Lanna and Helios, head east and check the forest as far as you can. Kyra, you and Rigel circle west and then south. Lanna, have Helios tell Cherish that she and Santos should sweep the town thoroughly and then circle outside the wall, looking for any signs. We'll join up by the main gate an hour after sunrise. If the gods are willing, we'll have found Janise well before then."

"Yessir," the riders replied.

Kyra patted Rigel's neck and turned west, while the others slogged north and east. At first, Konstantine wondered why Kyra, clearly the youngest of the group, had been given the largest area of ground to cover. It soon became apparent that Rigel was uniquely suited to the task of searching large areas.

While Stardust plowed through the snow toward the pass, and Helios lumbered a bit more swiftly to the east, Rigel vaulted to the top of the snowdrifts and sped west at an astonishing speed. The sleet pelting Stan's face felt like bee stings, and the wind threatened to rip the breath from his lungs.

"H-how. . . ?" he managed to gasp.

Kyra laughed, an incongruous sound in the smothering, frigid grayness. "All unicorns have gifts. Rigel can run like the wind and cross any terrain as though it were open ground. Hold tight and keep your eyes open, Stan. We'll need all six of our eyes to spot Janise in this tempest."

Konstantine did as he was told, clinging tight to the warm, muscular girl, and scanning in all directions as they rode. The village lights behind them became pale dots and then quickly vanished in the snow and darkness.

I could be a thousand miles from home, Stan thought. And, for a moment, he wished he were a thousand miles away. How wonderful to be on some great adventure with this unicorn rider girl! How wonderful to never have to return to the bleak days and dreary nights of Wolfnacht!

The wind and stinging snow soon cured Stan of his fancies. His toes and fingers quickly began to ache with the cold. To keep his mind off his frozen digits, he asked, "How does one become a unicorn rider?"

"Some enlist," Kyra said. "Others are conscripted. Still others, like me, are Chosen."

"What does that mean?"

"It means that we seem fated to be unicorn riders," she replied. "At some point in our lives, our mounts find us, and we never look back."

"So, Rigel found you?"

"Yes," the rider and her golden unicorn said in unison.

"How?"

Kyra didn't reply.

Rigel's deep voice broke the uncomfortable silence. "That's a tale for another time."

V. A Rider's Life

"Konstantine, do you know where we are?" Kyra asked.

Stan looked around. Impending dawn had brightened the surrounding wilderness, and through the swirling flakes he saw dark, mountainous shapes ahead. "We're nearing the western side of the valley—I think," he said.

"We'll stop a moment, check our bearings, and warm up, before circling south," Kyra said. Rigel slowed and settled lightly into the snow.

"I'm plenty warm," he remarked. The unicorn snorted and great clouds of steam rose into the snowy sky.

"Well, my limbs are stiff and cold, and I'm betting Konstantine's are, too," Kyra said.

"I'm fine," Stan insisted. "I can keep going."

Rigel snorted again.

"Take a few minutes to stretch," Kyra told Stan. She hopped off of Rigel's back and paced through the snow, swinging her arms vigorously.

Stan got down, nearly slipping, and did the same.

Kyra drew her sword and made a few practice cuts in the air. The weapon gleamed silver in the gray of the storm.

"Is it magical?" Stan asked, his eyes wide. His heart fluttered with the possibility.

"No," Kyra replied. "I'm not of high enough rank for magic— nor have I won such a weapon in combat. The blade is a silver alloy, though."

Konstantine's stomach growled, and he wished he had brought something to eat.

"All riders carry weapons of silver and iron," Rigel added. "In our jobs, we need such things."

"Yes, I understand," Stan said. Supposedly, weapons of silver or cold iron were more effective against the Enemy's forces.

"If I live long enough, I'll have better," Kyra mused. With a final flourish, she sheathed the sword at her belt.

Somehow, it had never really occurred to Stan just how dangerous this silver-haired girl's occupation was. Every day, she put her life in danger; every time she rode her golden unicorn, there was a chance she would never see another sunset. "*If I live long enough. . .*" The idea behind the words made Stan's chest tighten.

"I-I'm sure you'll be fine," he said. "You'll have plenty of time . . . I mean . . . I'm sure you'll have the best weapons one day." He smiled at her, but felt foolish.

"I'll settle for just living through the night," she replied. ". . . And finding Janise."

"Time to get moving," Rigel urged.

"Right," Kyra said. She mounted quickly and helped Stan up behind her. He clung tight, though her crossbow quiver felt cold and unyielding against his chest.

"Circle south and the back toward the city," she told her mount.

"I heard Volstag's plan," Rigel replied. "Did you think I'd forgotten?"

Again, she laughed.

Even though she's not much older than me, Konstantine thought, *she's used to danger*.

They galloped south, weaving back and forth across the tops of the drifts in a careful search pattern. For Stan, the world became a cold gray blur. The only thing that remained real to him was the girl and the thundering gallop of her steed. He found even this frigid existence preferable to his lowly life in Wolfnacht.

"Do you think . . ." he began. "Do you think *I* could join the cavalry?"

At first, he thought though Kyra hadn't heard him through the wind. A low neigh, like a chuckle, rumbled from Rigel's barrel-like chest.

"I'd like to see the world," Stan added, "or Atrios, anyway. And I'd like to fight evil. I know I'm young, but . . ."

"You're older than Kyra was when I met her," Rigel put in.

"I don't see why you couldn't," Kyra finally said. "Assuming any of us make it back to base, you're welcome to tag along. I can't promise you'll be accepted, but you can at least try."

Her answer made him feel even warmer than the closeness of her body. *To leave Wolfnacht! To strike out into the world and leave his dull life behind!*

"You'll have to stay alert if you want to join the cavalry," Rigel warned, breaking Stan's reverie.

"I will. I promise."

They rode silently for a while, as the snow-filled sky grew gradually lighter. The storm was abating as well; the howl of the wind no longer drowned out the blood pounding in Stan's frigid ears.

Kyra gazed at the sky, cursed, and said, "It's time to go back. Gods of Mercy, I was hoping we'd turn up some sign of her."

"Maybe the others have," Stan said hopefully.

"Helios and Lanna haven't," Rigel replied. "We would have heard."

The golden unicorn turned north and galloped back toward town. Soon, the jagged teeth of the palisade appeared through the blizzard. Beyond the wall crouched the dark houses of Wolfnacht.

"When's the eclipse?" Kyra asked.

"I don't know," Stan replied. "I didn't know about the festival at all until you arrived."

"No wonder he wants to leave home," Rigel mused.

Kyra patted the stallion on the neck as he ran. "Some are lucky enough to be born into their families," she said, "others have to find them."

"Which were you?" asked Stan.

"Both," she replied—and then fell silent once more.

When they reached the wall, they circled to the left. The storm had abated enough that they could see tracks around the palisade—but only the hoofprints of unicorns, no trace of human feet.

They circled west and soon spotted Santos and Apollonia riding toward them.

"Any sign of her?" Santos asked.

Kyra shook her head.

"That's bad," he said. "Helios told Apollonia that she and Lanna hadn't found anything either and said they were circling north to join Volstag and Stardust in searching near the pass."

Stan nodded understandingly and said, "Unicorn telepathy."

Santos raised an eyebrow at him.

"Konstantine is thinking of joining up," Kyra explained.

The curly haired rider and Apollonia regarded the boy skeptically. "Today's not a great time to enlist," Santos said, "but if this fool wants to stick his neck on the chopping block, who am I to argue?"

"I take it you didn't find any trace of Janise in town," Kyra said.

"Nothing—though the whole place seemed to be stirring as we rode out."

The festival, Nikolas thought. *It's almost time.*

"Any trouble getting through the gate?" Kyra asked Santos.

"No. That Nikolas guy opened it right up and smiled as we left."

"Let's hope our welcome back is equally warm," Rigel replied.

Stan doubted it would be, but he didn't say anything.

They kept riding north, circling the fifteen-foot-tall wooden walls, heading toward the main gate.

"Did the potion work?" Stan asked cautiously.

"Apollonia's living proof," Santos said, patting his mount's dappled shoulder. "Roj was coming around, too, when we left. He was making rumbles like he might join the search."

Kyra shook her head. "He should save his strength. If Volstag and the rest haven't found her—and I assume they haven't, since we haven't heard—I'm afraid there's not much hope."

Santos frowned. "Well, she couldn't just up and vanish."

"In weather like this, I'm afraid she could," Konstantine replied. "There was a woodcutter two years ago who went to fetch some logs. It was only a ten minute trip, but he never came back. And last week, old Sekta disappeared. The elders said she went to cut snow blossoms or mistletoe in the woods, but no one's seen her since."

"Maybe wolves got them," Santos suggested.

"There are no wolves around here," Stan said. "Not since Olen Wolfnacht's time."

Santos rubbed the dark stubble of his unshaven chin. "Wolves have good sense. Maybe they heard the Enemy coming and cleared out. If your people know what's good for them, they'll do the same."

"Aye," Kyra agreed.

"Maybe the magic ritual will work," Stan said. "Maybe Wolfnacht will be protected for another hundred years."

"Maybe," Santos agreed, though he didn't sound any more confident than Stan felt.

As they reached the front wall, a murmuring chant drifted out from inside the palisade. The riders stopped thirty yards from the gate and listened.

"Maybe they're starting the ceremony," Kyra suggested.

"The sun should just be coming over the forest," Stan said, peering east. Though the day had grow progressively brighter, and the blizzard had lessened, the distance still remained obscured by snowfall. They could see neither sunrise nor Wolfnacht Pass.

"Festivals usually start at the second bell of the morning," Stan said. "I'm surprised we didn't hear the first bell."

"Me, too," muttered Kyra, frowning.

The chant built, voices joining one another in a chorus of wailing.

"Sounds like they're having a right good time," Santos said.

Kyra appeared nervous; Stan felt it, too.

Suddenly, a scream pierced the rhythmic shouts. Kyra sat bolt upright, as did Santos. The unicorns turned their heads toward the main gate, and the riders' hands strayed to the hilts of their weapons.

A shiver ran down Konstantine's spine.

"What in the name of the Blessed Lady was that?" Santos asked.

"We should find out," Kyra said.

"Wait, I see something," Santos said. He pointed toward the mountains.

Out of the white distance, two riders appeared. Volstag and Stardust charged straight toward the gate, with Lanna and Helios following right behind. Helios stumbled through the drifting snow, struggling to keep up. Both riders and steeds were weary and battered.

Apollonia and Rigel rode out and met their comrades a half-mile from the town wall.

"The Enemy is through the pass!" Volstag announced breathlessly. "Keep riding! Back to the village!" The others formed in behind him and galloped back the way they'd come.

Stan peered into the snow, expecting to see undead swarming down from the mountains at any moment.

"They nearly took us while we searched for Janise," Lanna said. "We didn't see them coming through the snow."

"Didn't Stardust sense the danger?" Santos asked.

Volstag shook his head, and drips of sweat and melting snow fell from his salt-and-pepper hair. "There's so much danger all around us, her heightened senses are useless."

"We dealt the Enemy a blow before escaping," Lanna added, "but they won't be delayed long." Her shoulder was bleeding afresh, and she sported new cuts on her face, arms, and legs. A long purplish bruise swelled on the side of Helios' face. The unicorn blinked wearily, looking as though he might collapse at any moment.

That's why he didn't warn us telepathically, Stan thought. *The wound must have addled his brain.*

Helios struggled to stay on his feet as the group skidded to a halt before the wall.

"Open the gates!" Kyra called, rapping heavily on the wood with her fist.

"Open up! Let us in!" Stan added.

The bearded face of Nikolas poked up above the palisade.

"The Enemy is coming!" Volstag boomed. "We haven't much time!"

"You're right, you don't," Nikolas said. "You shouldn't have left. Especially not you, Stan."

"But we can help defend you!" Lanna said.

"Fools! You can't even defend yourselves!"

"You bastard!" Stan cried. "Let us in!"

"Too late . . . brother."

VI. Sacrifice

Nikolas sneered down at them mercilessly. Beyond the wall, the wailing chant of the villagers built to a fever pitch.

Then, a terrible, keening cry rose above the screams. The sound pierced Stan's heart, chilling him to the bottom of his soul. The unicorn riders looked as though they'd been struck physically.

"That's Cherish!" Lanna shouted.

"What's happening? What are you doing to her?" Santos yelled, his face flushing.

Nikolas shrugged and shook his head. "It doesn't matter," he said. "Not to you." As the bearded Wolfnachter turned away, Santos pulled out a crossbow and shot at him. The bolt flashed past Nikolas' head, brushing aside a stray lock of coarse black hair. Stan's brother laughed and vanished behind the palisade.

Bellowing with anger, Volstag and Stardust charged the gate. The silver mare lowered her head, and her spiral horn bit deep into the wood, passing straight through the three-inch thick boards. Splinters flew and the great doors shuddered with the impact, but the gate did not break. Stardust backed off to try another run. Volstag hefted his battle ax. Lanna drew her longbow. She and Santos scanned the wall for hostile villagers, giving their sergeant cover.

Again, Stardust crashed into the gates, and, this time, Volstag added a powerful blow from his ax. Again, the huge doors shuddered, but did not give way.

"It's not enough!" Santos said, almost spitting the words. "We'll never make it through in time." He and Apollonia backed away from the gate, eyeing the palisade.

Kyra and Rigel did the same. "Can you make it with two?" the warrior girl asked her golden mount.

"I think so," the unicorn replied. His gaze flashed from the wall to the newly healed scars on Apollonia's flank. The stallion seemed unsure whether the dappled mare was well enough for whatever they were about to attempt.

"What are we—?" Konstantine began.

"Hang on!" Kyra said.

With a sudden burst of speed, Rigel and Apollonia charged forward. They bounded deep into the trampled snow and then sprang into the air.

The unicorns sailed through the snowy sky as gracefully as birds. Rigel, Kyra, and Stan easily cleared the spiked tops of the palisade.

Stan glanced down and saw the startled face of his brother as Rigel soared overhead. The golden unicorn landed inside the wall, his hooves touching down lightly upon the snowy street.

Apollonia's leap didn't end as cleanly. Her back hooves clipped the top of the palisade and nearly took off Nikolas' head. Stan's brother threw himself out of the way just in time.

Apollonia landed awkwardly; her legs buckled and her hooves skidded across the avenue's slick surface. Santos held on, his expert riding keeping him on her back.

Rigel paused, waiting for the other two to recover.

"We're all right!" Santos called. "Keep going! I'll open the gate!"

Apollonia scrambled upright and turned toward the doors. As she did, Nikolas pulled out a shortbow and loosed an arrow at her.

The arrow missed the unicorn and lodged firmly in Santos' shoulder. The dark-haired rider grunted in pain, but managed not to fall off his steed. Santos whirled and fired his crossbow at Stan's brother; Nikolas ducked out of the way and reloaded his bow.

"Let me down!" Stan said, trying to wriggle off of Rigel's back. "I . . . I can help open the gate!"

"No!" Santos barked. "Kyra, take the boy with you! Have him guide you through the streets. He'd only get in the way here!" He swung his crossbow in a guarding motion and deflected Nikolas' second shot. The arrow skidded off of Apollonia's flank, tracing a line of crimson down her rump.

"Find Cherish!" Santos ordered. "Go!"

"Yes, Corporal!" Kyra replied. She tightened her legs around Rigel's sides and the golden unicorn shot down the street, away from the wall.

Nikolas wheeled and shot at Rigel's passengers, but his arrow fell harmlessly into a snow bank, several yards to their left.

"I can't believe he's shooting at us!" Stan muttered.

"Never mind about him," Rigel said. "Which way?"

"I-I don't know!"

"Think!" Kyra said, her voice calm but firm. "Where would they be holding the ceremony?"

"The wide avenue in front of the inn, maybe?" Stan suggested. "No, wait … the old church. Important ceremonies were always held by the church—at least until the priest died."

"Sacred ground," Kyra muttered. "A fitting place for whatever deviltry they're up to."

At that moment, the clouds overhead parted and golden rays of sunlight peeked through. The snow kept swirling, filling the air with dancing patterns of brilliant flakes.

Stan looked up and his eyes went wide. "The eclipse is coming!" he gasped. "Nyarra's nearly reached the sun—and I can hardly see her rings at all."

"The ringless moon blotting out the sun," Rigel whispered. "*Nyarra's Rebirth.*"

"Then the ceremony's reaching its climax!" Kyra exclaimed. "Quickly, Rigel!"

"Keep guiding me!" the stallion replied. His hooves kicked up small puffs of snow as he raced across the drift-covered streets.

The gloomy houses and alleys of Wolfnacht flew past. The village looked no more welcoming in the daylight than it had the previous night. Even the thick blanket of snow barely concealed the decay of the dying town.

"The church is there," Stan said, pointing. Ahead, a crooked alleyway opened up into a wide square in front of a dilapidated stone cathedral. The wailing song of the villagers grew to a deafening cacophony as the keening scream of the unicorn ceased.

Rigel skidded to a halt.

At the end of the alleyway, almost in the square, lay the body of Roj. His neck was twisted awkwardly and his eyes stared blankly up at the sky. A large, slushy pool of blood surrounded him, and snow dusted the young rider's ginger hair.

"Blessed Lady!" Kyra gasped.

She made to dismount, but Rigel said, "No. He's already dead."

Stan's heart went cold.

Kyra drew her sword; the silvery blade glistened in the sunlight.

Everyone in town was crowded into the square in front of the church. Every man, woman and child, held hands and wailed their ghastly festival chant. The five elders of Wolfnacht—Berman, Mapes, Zurko, Bev, and Thynes—stood on the decaying church's steps.

Between the elders and the crowd, on a makeshift stone altar, lay Cherish and Janise. The unicorn's blood stained the altar and splattered the snow-covered steps. Zurko, the butcher, held a knife made from an antler above his head. Gore from the blade dripped down his arm.

"The magic flows into the blade, multiplying the power!" Thynes announced, reading from an ancient scroll. "The protection of Wolfnacht will increase a thousand fold!" The aged scribe squinted up toward the sky. The clouds blew away and the blizzard ceased, revealing slender-ringed moon and blazing sun, nearly touching.

The wailing chant rose into a frenzied cheer as the rings tipped on edge, almost vanishing.

With a bellow of rage, Rigel leaped over Roj's body and charged.

The crowd wheeled as the unicorn thundered into the square. Some of the villagers stopped their chant and screamed in terror, but Mapes thrust out her bony hands and shouted, "Stop!"

Rigel skidded to a stop, kicking up a huge spray of slush. Kyra jerked forward and nearly fell from his back. Konstantine held on for dear life; it felt as though they had been struck by a powerful gust of wind.

Above them, the moon and the sun kissed. Nyarra's rings were a thin line now, and the satellite's cloudy face grew darker by the moment. The sky also darkened, not from the storm clouds looming around the perimeter of the village, but from the start of the eclipse.

Elder Berman grinned with satisfaction. "There's no need for further violence," he purred. "We warned you that we didn't want your help. Leave this place while you still can."

"You killed Cherish!" Rigel neighed.

"And Roj!" Kyra added.

"He resisted," Mapes said. "We can't let anyone interfere with the ritual—not after all these months we've spent planning."

"It was unfortunate," added Berman. "Your friend didn't have to die. One sacrifice would have been enough. We had intended to use one of our own . . ." Here, he glanced at an old woman in the crowd.

Sekta, Stan realized—the old woman who had vanished into the woods.

". . . Then you riders showed up," Berman continued, "with a girl who was nearly gone anyway. A much better sacrifice, I think you'll agree. The power of the unicorn was merely a bonus."

Rigel neighed and pawed the air, but he remained stuck against Mapes' invisible wall; try as they might, the unicorn and his riders could not move forward.

"The girl's blood is perfect," Bev, the herbalist, said. "She is young and brave, and her connection to the unicorns makes her much better to invoke Olen Wolfnacht's protection." Her gray eyes sparkled. "No offense, Sekta."

The ancient woman smiled a toothless smile and bowed in return.

"I can't believe the riders were trying to protect you!" Stan blurted.

Berman scoffed. "We don't need their protection," he said. "The ritual of Wolfnacht is all we need. Then we will be strong."

"Don't you understand?" Kyra said, pleading. "This is wrong! Your ritual has been perverted. You people aren't fighting the Enemy—you're *joining* the Enemy! Please, let Janise go!"

All five elders laughed.

Kyra sheathed her sword. "What about you, Stan?" she asked coldly. "Do you want to join your people?"

Stan's guts twisted and roiled. "I'm with you now, not them," he replied.

"Make sure you stay that way," Rigel whispered.

With one lightning swift move, Kyra drew her crossbow and shot. Her silver-tipped bolt streaked through the invisible barrier and buried itself in Zurko's chest. The butcher gasped and crumpled to the stairs, dead. Kyra reloaded.

"Back off! All of you! Now!" she snarled. "Stand away from Janise! I will kill every one of you if you try to harm her!"

The elders stood stunned for a moment, and the chanting of the crowd died away. Then, with a howl of incoherent rage, the mob surged toward the unicorn riders.

"Should I retreat into the alley?" Rigel asked. "It will be easier to defend."

"No!" Kyra replied. "We need to get to Janise!" She drew a bead on Mapes and shot again, but a villager threw himself in front of the bolt and died in the witch's stead. Mapes and the remaining elders scrambled to retrieve Zurko's fallen sacrificial dagger.

Rigel lunged into the crowd. Kyra quickly traded her crossbow for her sword and began slashing. The villagers stayed away from the silvery blade, but kept the unicorn and rider hemmed in, refusing to let the rescuers near the church steps.

Stan held on for dear life. The people of Wolfnacht, once his friends, clawed at him, trying to pull him and Kyra from Rigel's back. Stan beat them back with his fists, bruising his fingers and bloodying his knuckles, but the mob kept coming.

Not all the villagers were attacking the riders, though. Some began chanting again as the four remaining elders resumed the ceremony. Berman proudly clutched the sacrificial knife.

Tied to the altar, Janise roused from her stupor and screamed, her cry rising above the rhythmic wails of the entranced villagers.

Just then, Volstag, Lanna, Santos, and their unicorns thundered out of the alley and into the square. They joined the melee, but Kyra and her friends remained massively outnumbered.

The moon blotted out the sun and Nyarra's Rebirth began; the satellite's rings completed turning edge on and became invisible in the growing darkness.

Berman raised the antler knife high and plunged it into Janise's chest, stilling her screams forever.

VII. Wolfnacht

Kyra and Stan both shouted, "No!"

The mob roared with triumph. As the echoes of the victory cry died away, the people of Wolfnacht began to change.

Their wailing chants became an obscene chorus of pain and delight. The villagers transformed, their bodies twisting and growing more muscular. Their faces elongated, their noses became snouts, and their ears grew tall and pointed. They ripped apart their confining clothes with long, sharp talons. Their teeth became fangs, and coarse fur sprouted from every inch of their skin.

In a frenzy, the villagers' crouched forms capered and loped wildly around the square. They turned their faces to the eclipsed moon and howled their exultation.

"Gods of Wrath and Mercy!" Volstag whispered.

The villagers who had been trampled under the unicorns' hooves wrenched themselves to their feet as their broken bones knitted back into place.

"Werewolves!" Santos cried.

"Run!" screamed Lanna. "We have to get out! There's nothing we can do here now!"

"Nothing but die!" growled the wolf-like thing who had once been Thynes.

He leaped at Lanna and Helios, but the half-elf wheeled and put a silver-tipped arrow through his eye. The scribe fell to the ground, twitching; he transformed back into a man as he died.

A grim smile crossed Volstag's face. "At least the tried-and-true methods still work."

The pack howled with anger and leapt after the fleeing riders.

"Go! Go! Go!" Santos yelled.

"That way!" Konstantine called, pointing. Werewolves already clogged the alley the riders had used to enter the square, so Stan picked a wide street leading toward the gates.

Kyra glanced over her shoulder at him, trying to read his intent. "Do it!" she cried to the rest and urged Rigel in the direction Stan indicated. The others galloped toward the avenue, too. Volstag and Stardust led the way. Rigel and Apollonia fell in behind, with Helios—still sporting wounds from his fight in the pass earlier—and Lanna bringing up the rear.

The mob swarmed in around the cavalry, slashing with wolfish claws, nipping at the unicorns' hindquarters. The werewolves were clumsy and slow; they hadn't yet adjusted to their new shapes, and this worked in the riders' favor.

A hairy monster who had once been Elder Bev jumped out in front of Stardust. Volstag whirled his ax and sliced the former herbalist in two. Stardust trampled both halves of the elder into the snow.

Kyra's sword described a deadly arc, protecting her, Stan, and Rigel. The weapon's silver blade bit through hairy wolf skin, leaving steaming gashes in supernatural flesh. The townsfolk howled in pain and anger. Even as they backed away from Kyra's weapon, they clawed at her, trying to drag her, Rigel, and Stan down.

"Are you all right, Konstantine?" Kyra asked as the cavalry galloped out of the square.

Stan felt far from all right. His heart was pounding, sweat drenched every inch of his body, and he feared he might vomit. "I'm fine," he gasped. "I don't think the transformation spell affected me." He hoped he was telling the truth.

"Good," she said. "Just hang onto me. I'll get you out of this. I promise."

"And don't let them bite you," Rigel cautioned. "Anyone surviving a werewolf bite becomes a werewolf—and there's no magic in the World-Sea that will save you."

Stan swallowed, hardly daring to glance back at the rabid mob pursuing them.

Because the town's residents had gathered in the square for the ceremony, all the werewolves were behind the cavalry. No lupine shapes sprang out to bar the riders' way as the unicorns galloped down the deserted, snowy streets of Wolfnacht.

But the villagers knew the town better than the Atrian patrol, and it didn't take long for the werewolves to adjust to their new forms. The transformed villagers quickly organized into several smaller packs and raced after the fugitives. The alleyways echoed with their howls.

Kyra pulled a silver dagger from her boot. "Use this to protect yourself," she said, handing the blade Konstantine as they rushed headlong through the town.

Stan reached for it, but the dagger slipped through his fingers. He fumbled for the blade, bounced it off of Rigel's flank, and snatched it up just before it tumbled to the street.

"Watch it!" Rigel snapped.

"Sorry," Stan replied. He smoothed the golden coat on Rigel's hindquarters, just to make sure he hadn't done any harm. As he glanced back, his blood ran cold.

Lanna and Helios, still suffering from earlier wounds, had fallen behind the rest of the riders. As Stan watched in horror, the hideous wolfpack caught up with the half-elf and her mount.

At the last instant, Helios wheeled and charged full force into the hairy, rampaging mob. Wolflike bodies scattered before the unicorn's stabbing horn and trampling hooves. Lanna's longsword flashed in the eclipse-born darkness, and several werewolves fell dead, but twice as many leaped forward to take their place.

"Lanna!" Stan screamed. "They've got Lanna and Helios!"

Kyra and the others wheeled around, startled. They would have turned to help, but Lanna shouted, "Flee! Run while you still can!" Then clawed hands fastened onto her tunic and dragged the half-elf from the saddle. An instant later, the pack pulled down Helios, too.

As the unicorn disappeared into the ravenous mob, pain stabbed through Stan's head. For a moment, he clearly heard the telepathic voice of Helios in his mind.

"*Don't let our sacrifice be in vain!*" the unicorn whinnied.

Volstag screamed in incoherent rage and yelled, "Ride for all you're worth!" He and Stardust thundered away from the pack.

"Gods curse this town and everyone in it!" Santos cried, following. Kyra tightened her grip on her sword and rode on.

Hot tears clouded Stan's vision. He could barely make out the palisade wall as the remaining riders rushed toward the half-opened gate. Beyond the portal, human-like shapes shambled in the snowy darkness—not werewolves, but something else. Stan's guts twisted as he realized that the true Enemy had finally arrived.

"Sergeant. . . !" Kyra began; she also had spotted the new menace.

"I see them," Volstag replied. "Form up! We'll charge straight through if we have to. There's nothing more we can do here. We need to make it back to base and brief the colonel." He gazed sternly at both Kyra and Santos. "No matter what happens, keep riding. That's an order!"

Both riders nodded. Only a dozen yards separated the three cavalry troopers from the gate when, suddenly, the great doors began to swing shut.

"It's a trap!" Santos cried.

As he said it, werewolves sprang up from their hiding places on the parapet walkway. Many of the transformed monsters were indistinguishable from enormous wolves; others retained a hideous mix of human and wolf traits. A half-dozen wolfmen clutched shortbows in their feral claws.

"Shoot!" hissed one of the damnable creatures.

The wolfman archers fired as one. Their black-shafted arrows streaked through the air. At the last instant, Apollonia leapt forward, shielding her comrades from the hail of deadly shafts.

The arrows struck the unicorn's dappled body with a series of sickening thuds. Apollonia crashed to the ground, but stumbled to her feet once more.

"Again!" hissed the lead monster. Stan's heart nearly ripped in two as he recognized the voice and the twisted visage of his brother, Nikolas.

Again, Apollonia leaped and took the full brunt of the arrow fire. Santos batted aside two of the arrows with his sword, but another struck him in the chest, and three more sank into his unicorn.

"Go!" Santos wailed and he and Apollonia tumbled into the snow.

Only a slender gap remained between the gates, but Stardust and Volstag didn't slow. They charged headlong into the great doors. Stardust lowered her head, and her spiral horn gleamed golden in the dim light of the eclipse; Volstag brandished his ax.

The pair met the huge wooden doors head on. Splinters filled the air, and metal groaned and snapped as the impact wrenched the gates from their hinges. Stardust staggered through the portal and into the snow-covered landscape beyond.

Kyra and Rigel followed, dragging Konstantine with them. The last thing Stan saw as they exited Wolfnacht was Santos and Apollonia lying unmoving in the street, pinioned with black-fletched arrows. Werewolf archers jumped down from the palisade and began tearing at the bodies.

Stan turned away, but the sights ahead appeared just as dire. During the blizzard, the Enemy's forces—zombies, gaunts, ghouls, and creatures far worse—had found their way through the pass. Now the undead surrounded the village, blocking the riders' escape. Konstantine turned this way and that, desperately seeking a way out, knowing that the werewolves would soon be on their heels once more.

Dozens of zombies penned in the two remaining unicorns. The animated corpses staggered through the snow, feeling neither the cold nor the decay of their own flesh. More undead streamed down from the pass, which remained hidden in the blowing snow and eclipse-born darkness. To Stan's frightened eyes, the stream of supernatural monsters looked endless.

Volstag chopped down the first two zombies in his way; Stardust skewered another, tossed it into the air, and trampled two more. "Go west!" the sergeant called to Kyra. "Then circle south and back to base. If we ride directly east, they'll catch us in the forest."

Kyra didn't reply, but responded by cutting down a zombie blocking their escape. Rigel charged westward, but the zombies' attacks kept him bogged down in the snow. Konstantine held onto the warrior girl with one hand and kept a tight grip on his silver knife with the other. He seldom swung at their enemies, for fear of losing his weapon. Instead, he concentrated on keeping out of the way of the monsters' attacks.

"Gods curse it!" Volstag cried. Stardust surged toward Rigel, but she was nowhere as nimble as Kyra's golden unicorn. Battering through the gate and her wounds from the search had taken a toll on the silver mare. The zombies pressed in around her, and the faster-moving gaunts slashed at her flanks. Even Volstag's lighting-quick ax couldn't fend off every attack.

A knife-wielding gaunt leapt forward and gouged a long cut in Volstag's thigh. The sergeant grunted in pain, as the dagger skidded off his leg and plunged into Stardust's side. The unicorn wailed in agony.

"Volstag!" Kyra shouted. "Stardust!"

Just then, a pack of werewolves burst out of the city and joined the attack. Volstag and his steed had lagged behind Kyra and Rigel, and the werewolves ran straight for the wounded unicorn.

Spotting the enemy reinforcements, Volstag caught Kyra's eye and hissed, "Don't you *dare* stop, Private!"

With a mighty roar, he swung his silver-bladed ax in a huge circle. The blade decapitated one werewolf and cut the arm off another. Five more zombies fell to Stardust's hooves and horn, but the undead and the werewolves kept coming.

"Gods of Mercy, help us!" Kyra cried. If the gods were listening, they didn't respond to Kyra's plea. Stan bit his lip so hard that he tasted blood.

He kicked away a zombie clawing at Rigel's side. Stan's boot crushed the animated corpse's face, and it fell back into the snow with a sickening splash. Rigel stomped two more undead into rotting jelly. Then, as Kyra sliced off three clawing hands, the golden unicorn sprang free.

Suddenly, Rigel was on top of the snow pack, racing west along the wall, toward freedom. Few zombies stood in their way, and the unicorn batted those aside with horn and hoof.

Behind them, the forces of the Enemy surrounded Volstag and Stardust and dragged them down. The sergeant and his mount kept fighting, even as the monsters tore them to pieces.

"No!" Kyra cried, tears streaming down her face. "NO! Rigel, turn back!"

Rigel kept running.

As the echo of Kyra's anguished cry died away, a hairy shape leapt from the top of the wall. The creature landed on Kyra and Stan, knocking them from Rigel's back. The force of the blow sent the unicorn tumbling. The great golden steed rolled twice and crashed heavily into the palisade wall.

The rider, the adolescent, and the monster landed hard. Snow burst up around them in a blinding cloud of frigid crystals. Kyra rolled to her feet, groping for her dropped sword; the werewolf rose quickly as well. Stan blinked and shook his head, trying to clear his vision. He stumbled toward where Rigel lay.

"Don't leave yet, brother," the werewolf growled. A casual swipe of his claw sent Konstantine sprawling.

Kyra grabbed her sword, but Nikolas lunged at her before she could raise it. He batted the sword from her hand and snapped at her face. Kyra ducked aside; the wolf's slavering teeth missed her throat by inches.

She drew her iron-bladed knife from her boot sheath and stabbed it deep into Nikolas' gut. The wolfman howled with anguish, but he did not die. He swung wildly and his forearm crashed into Kyra's chest, sending her sprawling.

She landed two yards away, stunned and half buried in a snow drift. Nikolas laughed, pulled her dagger out of his stomach, and tossed it aside.

"The power of Wolfnacht is stronger than unicorn magic," he sneered.

Desperately, Stan sprang to his feet. As Nikolas leapt for the fallen rider, Stan jumped between them. Kyra's silver dagger remained tightly clutched in the Stan's hand. He tried to bring the weapon around, but Nikolas smashed full-force into him.

Something snapped inside Stan's chest, and his body exploded with pain. The brothers crashed into the snow. The dagger slipped from Stan's fingers, landing in the drift beside Kyra. Nikolas howled with rage, trying to rip himself free of his brother's entangling body.

Bleary-eyed, Kyra scooped up the dagger and lunged. Her thrust brushed past Stan's neck and sunk into Nikolas' chest, just below the left shoulder. The werewolf howled and staggered back, but, again, he didn't die. He clutched the smoking wound, hatred blazing in his feral, red eyes.

Stan suddenly realized that the undead had caught up to them during the fight. The zombies and gaunts surrounded them, waiting to feast once the werewolf had slain the rider and her foolish companion. Outside the circle, more undead shambled forward like an endless, rotting tide. Behind them came the werewolves of Wolfnacht.

Stan collapsed in the snow, his strength exhausted, but Kyra staggered to her feet. Her blue eyes blazed as she stared at Nikolas.

"Come on, then!" she gasped, the silver dagger clenched tight in her fist. "Let's finish this!"

"Yes," Nikolas snarled. "Let's!"

Suddenly, Rigel burst into the circle of undead. He decapitated a zombie with his horn and trampled three more as he raced to his rider.

"Come on!" Kyra cried. She leaped onto Rigel's back and extended her hand to Konstantine.

Stan reached out, his fingers brushed hers . . .

Kyra seized him in her firm grip and pulled him onto the back of her galloping steed. With a mighty leap, Rigel cleared the ring of monsters and landed atop the snow a half-dozen yards away.

"After them!" Nikolas howled.

Heart pounding, Stan glanced back at their pursuers. The zombies were no match for Rigel's speed, nor were the other undead. The werewolves were much faster, though. A dozen of them, their fur matted with blood, raced after the unicorn riders.

Rigel was bruised and scraped, and he limped slightly as he broke into a gallop.

Can he outrun them? Stan wondered. As the walls of Wolfnacht faded into the snowy gloom, the howling werewolves drew closer to their prey—ever closer.

Kyra unlimbered her crossbow and took careful aim.

Twang! A silver bolt pierced the eye of the lead wolf and he tumbled across the snow, dead.

A hopeful grin crept over Stan's face.

"Don't smile yet," she said. "There are more werewolves than I have crossbow bolts."

As she spoke, the landscape around them suddenly grew brighter.

Stan turned his face to the sky. "The eclipse is ending!" he cried.

The pursuing werewolves fell, a twisting heap of fur and contorting limbs. They screamed hideously as their bodies changed back into human form.

"You prayed for a miracle," Rigel's deep voice rumbled. "Looks like you got it."

"The gods help those who help themselves," Kyra replied.

"Should we go back and finish them off?" the unicorn asked.

Kyra shook her head. "We can't chance it. Sunlight won't stop those zombies from killing us, even if it does slow down the gaunts and the ghouls. Besides, Sergeant Volstag ordered us back to base." She choked back a sob. "It was his last order, and I'll be damned if we're not going to carry it out."

Rigel kept running. After a time, his fatigue seemed to lessen and his pace evened out. Stan slumped against Kyra, every muscle in his body aching, his brain afire with horrible memories of everything they'd been through during the past day.

Just as he began to drowse, Rigel cantered to a stop.

"What is it?" Stan asked, blinking. After the gloom of the storm and the eclipse, the sunlight was almost unbearably bright.

"We need to rest," Kyra said, "at least for a moment." She climbed down from Rigel's back and stretched her limbs. Stan dismounted and did the same.

They'd stopped in a small clearing in the lee of a stand of sturdy pine trees. The wind had blown the earth bare, here, and Rigel dipped his head to lick at the frozen grass.

Kyra removed three strips of dried meat from her rucksack. "Want some?" she asked.

"Sure," Stan replied. She tossed the backpack to him, and he stopped to retrieve it.

When he stood again, she had her crossbow out and a silver bolt loaded.

He stared behind them, terrified that—somehow—they had been followed. "What is it?" he asked desperately. "Are they coming?"

"No," she replied in a soft voice. "Just a precaution. Are you all right, Konstantine?" She was gazing at his ribs, just below his left shoulder.

Stan looked down and saw dried blood amid the torn fabric. A chill ran down his spine. "I'm fine," he said. "It's nothing."

The unicorn stopped browsing and asked, "When did you get that wound, Konstantine?"

"I-I don't know," Stan said. "Sometime during the fight, I guess. I don't remember."

"It looks like a bite," the unicorn observed. "A wolf bite."

Kyra aimed her crossbow at Stan's chest.

Stan dropped her pack onto the frozen grass. "Kyra," he said, pleading, "it's *me*."

"Did he bite you?" Kyra asked, her voice flat and emotionless. "Did Nikolas bite you?"

"I . . . I don't know. Maybe. I was trying to save you. Remember? I saved your life!"

"I know you did, Konstantine," she said, "and I'm sorry."

"Kyra, I could never hurt you—or Rigel. I wouldn't hurt anyone! I want to be a unicorn rider!"

"I'm afraid that's impossible now," she said.

"No it isn't!" Stan barked. "I'm not like the rest! Even before you came, I wasn't like the others! I didn't change when they did! I'm one of *you*—not one of them!

She pointed the crossbow straight at his heart.

"Kyra, please! I'm your friend!" Tears streamed down his face and the blood pounded hot in his ears. "You said you'd get me out of this! You promised!"

Rigel lowered his horn and prepared to charge.

Stan slumped to his knees and sobbed, "You promised!"

Slowly, Kyra lowered her crossbow. "I remember."

Rigel frowned at her and shook his mane. "This is probably a mistake."

116

"Time will tell," the silver-haired rider replied. She stowed her weapon and climbed up on her unicorn's back.

Stan gazed up at her, and she held out her hand.

"Come on," she said. "We've a long way yet to ride."

ABOUT THE STORIES

Both novellas came about as ideas for the *Blue Kingdoms: Shades & Specters* anthology. I wasn't sure which tale I wanted to use, so I decided to write them both.

Short stories are always tricky for me; I'm more comfortable with longer formats. One of the ways I've developed to cope with this is to *not* outline before I write. I dash off a few notes, a few characters, and then I go.

From the length of the notes on these tales, I should have known that they weren't going to fit the 4000-6000-word format I'd assigned to the anthology. Heck, when all was said and done, they weren't even going to fit the 8000-10,000-word format of my last Blue Kingdoms "short."

But I didn't realize that when I decided to write *Festival at Wolfnacht*. I chose to do *Wolfnacht* first because I had a feeling—accurate, as it turned out—that the other contributing authors for *Specters* were going to turn in sea-faring tales.

That was fine, and Jean Rabe (my co-editor) and I like to let contributors have their rein. The Blue Kingdoms setting is more than just an ocean-covered world, so I wanted to include at least one story set far from the shores of the World-Sea. I thought that *Wolfnacht,* mired in the snowy mountains, would be a good break from ship-bound tales.

Horror stories are tricky to write. Both of these are of the Ten Little Indians variety—that is, they build suspense by bumping off characters as they go, until the reader (hopefully) doesn't know who will die next.

So, I needed a fistful of characters for *Wolfnacht*. That meant a good number of both riders (as victims) and townsfolk (to change into bad guys at the story's climax). *The Blood-Red Isle* faced a similar "suspense through attrition" problem, and I arrived at a similar boatload-of-characters solution.

Silly me. The number of characters in the story notes should have been my second hint that neither tale would end up short.

Wolfnacht originated with an image in my head of a werewolf and unicorn fighting in the snow. Not quite the same image as the cover of this volume, but enough to instill in me a strong desire to write.

I had been itching to do a Unicorn Cavalry story for some time. I've got a cavalry trilogy in the works, and I wanted to "warm up" some of the characters from that proposal. *Festival at Wolfnacht* serves as kind of a prelude to that upcoming arc. Of course, now that I've written *Wolfnacht*, I see that I could expand the novella into a full-length book of its own, too.

Ideas beget more ideas; which is another reason that short stories are tricky for me.

In any case, I hope you've enjoyed my unicorns versus werewolves and zombies epic. (Drop me a line at my Yahoo group and let me know.)

As I worked on *Wolfnacht* I realized that it was going to be too long for the anthology. More pages means more cost, and—as the publisher of Walkabout Publishing—I wanted to keep the anthology's price at $15 or less.

No problem, I thought. *I'll just finish* Wolfnacht *and move on to* Blood-Red Isle.

Good plan. It meant adding another island yarn to what was looking like a collection of sea-faring spooky stories, but so what? *Pirates of the Blue Kingdoms* had done well enough. No reason not to give the public more salty adventures.

Blood-Red Isle also began with a picture in my head—the image of the rotting, vine-covered corpse of Sanguinarre rising amid the wreckage of her throne room. I'm a visual guy (I majored in Fine Arts), and movies and illustrations have always been a strong influence on my work.

So, off I went again, aiming for that picture in my head.

About half way through *Blood-Red Isle* I realized that it, too, was going to be too long for the anthology. I'd written over 8000 words, and I still hadn't gotten to Sanguinarre's palace where the climax of the story takes place.

Then I had a brainstorm; I could cut *Blood-Red Isle* in half, re-start with my doomed characters already *in* the palace (thus avoiding the "island story" patina), and then continue to the end.

I inserted some judicious recapping (removed from this version of the story) after the "break," and . . . *Voila!* I now had a story the right length for the *Specters* collection, "Court of the Blood-Red Queen."

I still liked the first half of the story, though. It had a lot of character development and helped build to the Ten Little Indians-style horror payoff.

What to do? I'd "uncovered" two novella-length epics when all I really needed was a short.

Then it hit me. I could combine both of these spooky tales into a bone-chilling book of their own.

That way, people who like "Queen" in the anthology can check out the longer version of the story in this volume, and new readers get the full-length heart-pounding impact of both tales.

It seemed a perfect solution.

So, I created an attention-getting title, whipped up a new cover, and set the type. (Fortunately, my printer is very understanding.)

You hold the result in your hands—just in time for the holiday.

Happy Halloween.

ABOUT THE AUTHOR

Stephen D. Sullivan has been a professional writer, illustrator, and monster-maker since 1980. He is the author of more than thirty published novels and numerous comic books. His recent projects include *Martian Knights, Spider Riders,* and *Iron Man.* He has won the **Origins Award**—adventure gaming's highest honor—twice, first for his samurai fantasy novel *The Lion,* and later for his Mage Knight short story "Podo and the Magic Shield." His novel, *Dragonlance: Warrior's Heart,* was nominated for a 2006 Scribe Award. The second book in that trilogy, *Dragonlance: Warrior's Blood* was cited by the *Detroit Free Press* as a novel Harry Potter fans would enjoy. Steve's upcoming books include *Frost Harrow: Scream Lover, A Season of Fear,* and the final book in the Catriona trilogy, *Dragonlance: Warrior's Bones.* Steve lives in haunted Frosthaven, Wisconsin, with his wife and two children. More information about Steve and his work can be found at www.stephendsullivan.com.

Other Walkabout Publishing Books by
Stephen D. Sullivan

Martian Knights & Other Tales
Luck o' the Irish
Frost Harrow: Scream Lover (2011)
Tournament of Death (Now free online!)

And from other publishers:
Dragonlance: The Dragon Isles
Dragonlance: The Dying Kingdom
Dragonlance: Warrior's Heart
Dragonlance: Warrior's Blood
Dragonlance: Warrior's Bones
Iron Man: The Junior Novel
Thunderbirds: The Junior Novel
Fantastic 4: The Junior Novel
Elektra: The Junior Novel
The Spider Riders trilogy
Legend of the Five Rings:
The Scorpion
The Phoenix
The Lion

Other Blue Kingdoms Books:

Pirates of the Blue Kingdoms
Blue Kingdoms: Buxom Buccaneers
Blue Kingdoms: Shades & Specters
Blue Kingdoms: Mages & Magic

Available from www.walkaboutpublishing.com.

WALKABOUT PUBLISHING
Great stories by great authors.

Robert E. Vardeman—Michael A. Stackpole—Marc Tassin—James M. Ward
Lorelei Shannon—Dean Leggett—Kathleen Watness—Paul Genesse
Jason Mical—Kelly Swails—Sabrina Klein—Kerrie Hughes—John Helfers
Brandie Tarvin—Donald J. Bingle—Tim Wagonner—Anton Strout
E. Readicker-Henderson—Wes Nicholson—Linda P. Baker—Steven Saus
J. Robert King—Chris Pierson—Daniel Meyers—Elizabeth A. Vaughan
Richard Lee Byers—Jennifer Brozek—Brad Beaulieu—Dylan Birtolo
Paul McComas—William F. Nolan—Annette Leggett—Donald J. Bingle
Stephen D. Sullivan—Jean Rabe—And More!

Pirates of the Blue Kingdoms • Blue Kingdoms: Buxom Buccaneers
Blue Kingdoms: Shades & Specters • Blue Kingdoms: Mages & Magic
Zombies, Werewolves, & Unicorns • Stalking the Wild Hare
Luck o' the Irish • Martian Knights & Other Tales
Stories from Desert Bob's Reptile Ranch • Unforgettable
This and That and Tales About Cats • Uncanny Encounters: Roswell
Under the Protection of the Cow Demon • *And More!*

Walkabout Publishing
P.O. Box 151 • Kansasville, WI 53139
www.walkaboutpublishing.com
Official Home of the Blue Kingdoms.

www.ingramcontent.com/pod-product-compliance
Lightning Source LLC
Chambersburg PA
CBHW070754120626
46557CB00002B/592

The Fanatics
By
Nishoni Lynn Harvey

Word of His Mouth Publishers
Mooresboro, NC

All Scripture quotations are taken from the **King James Version** of the Bible.

ISBN: 978-0-9856042-1-9
Printed in the United States of America
©2012 Nishoni Lynn Harvey

Cover art by George Nuhrah

Word of His Mouth Publishers
PO Box 256
Mooresboro, NC 28114

To order more copies of this book please call 704-477-5439 or visit our web page at www.wordofhismouth.com.

All rights reserved. No part of this publication may be reproduced, in any form, without the prior written permission of the publisher except for quotations in printed reviews.